***Damnation,* what was it about this woman?**

Her exceptional figure? Her sharp wit? That glossy honey-blond hair?

Yes, yes and yes. And something more. Something that gnawed at him whenever he woke and wondered in the still dead of night.

The remnants of a need to tame her?

No, submission wasn't the prize. He'd never had the desire to tame any woman—only enjoy them. Spoil them. In his younger days the world had seemed full of alluring possibilities. Then his offshore oil and gas support company had taken off *and* he'd met Eden—a woman who possessed the contradictory seeds of both natural innocence and darkest temptation…a curious and, as it had turned out, addictive combination.

Time to face facts. The memory of that woman still had him by the horns, and that was far from acceptable. But there was a remedy—one simple answer to one simple question. When he had that he could put that nameless ghost to bed and Eden Foley out of his mind for good.

We can't help but love a bad boy!

The wicked glint in his eye…the rebellious streak that's a mile wide. His untamed unpredictability. The way he'll always get what he wants, on his own terms. The sheer confidence, charisma and barefaced charm of the guy.…

In this new miniseries from
Harlequin Presents®, these heroes
have all that—and a lot more besides!
They're

Wild, Wealthy and Wickedly Sexy!

Don't miss it—because in these hot new stories, bad is definitely better!

Robyn Grady

DEVIL IN A
DARK BLUE SUIT

UNTAMED
BILLIONAIRES

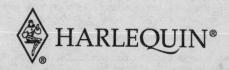

HARLEQUIN®

TORONTO • NEW YORK • LONDON
AMSTERDAM • PARIS • SYDNEY • HAMBURG
STOCKHOLM • ATHENS • TOKYO • MILAN • MADRID
PRAGUE • WARSAW • BUDAPEST • AUCKLAND

Recycling programs
for this product may
not exist in your area.

ISBN-13: 978-0-373-12881-5

DEVIL IN A DARK BLUE SUIT

First North American Publication 2009.

Copyright © 2009 by Robyn Grady.

www.eHarlequin.com

Printed in U.S.A.

All about the author…
Robyn Grady

One Christmas long ago, **ROBYN GRADY** received a book from her big sister and immediately fell in love with the story of Cinderella. Sprinklings of magic, deepest wishes coming true—she was hooked! Picture books with glass slippers later gave way to romance novels and, more recently, the real-life dream of writing for Harlequin Books.

After a fifteen-year career in television, Robyn met her own modern-day hero. They live on Australia's Sunshine Coast with their three little princesses, two poodles and a cat called Tinkie. Robyn loves new shoes, worn jeans, lunches at Moffat Beach and hanging out with her friends on eHarlequin.com. Learn about her latest releases at www.robyngrady.com, and don't forget to say hi. She'd love to hear from you!

With thanks to Qantas pilot,
Bruce "Ramjet" Rattle.

And my editor, Kimberley Young, for helping
me to achieve my best every time.

CHAPTER ONE

THE almighty crack of shattering glass sent Eden Foley's heart shooting like a bullet to her throat. 'Flight or fight' reflex pushed her to her feet as the Swarovski chandelier seemed to jingle overhead and the entire room jostled and gasped.

Good Lord! Had someone dropped a bomb on Sydney central?

Heartbeat racing, Eden peered out beyond the restaurant's massive glass frontage. Outside, stooped on the footpath, a woman gripped a baseball bat. A luxury sports car parked on the kerb glistened with the litter of its smashed windscreen. Now the woman swung again, ready to go to town on the gleaming black bonnet.

Her outfit might've been a nightdress, floating out when she put her all into the next big blow. As a boutique owner, Eden conceded that retro florals were in this season. Bad language and gnashing teeth were not.

At the same time the bat *thwacked* the bonnet, a tall, impressively built man ripped around the back of the car. With an effortless motion, he wrested the weapon from the attacker. Then, to block and shield some curious passersby, he stretched out his free arm. Like the closing scene from a thriller, a police car screeched up, its high-pitched siren cranking Eden's nerves up another notch. Two officers bounded out as the woman in her flowery garb crumpled, a sobbing mess, to the ground.

Weak with relief, Eden withered into her seat.

She knew the darkly attractive owner of that car. He was her luncheon date. A lifetime ago he'd swept her off her feet. For four blissful months she'd come alive and apart in Devlin Stone's arms.

Although their affair had ended badly, she wouldn't deny that they'd shared a special kind of bond—a connection a young woman with stars in her eyes had believed would last for ever. Six weeks ago Eden's sister had fallen into a similar trap. Sabrina had begun dating Devlin's younger brother, the well-publicised playboy, Nathan Stone.

Just as Devlin had cut Eden loose when his interest in her had waned, so too would bad-boy Nathan dump poor Sabrina when he'd had his fill of her. Hoping Sabrina would listen to reason and accept that her love affair would be short-lived was a waste of time. Having sampled the delights of a Stone herself, Eden knew from experience how hard facing facts could be. Still, Eden couldn't—and *wouldn't*—stand by and wait for her little sister's heart to be crushed.

The only likely solution lay in appealing to Devlin's compassionate side, asking him to speak with Nathan, as only a big brother could. Someone had to ask Nathan to let Sabrina off the hook—and *now*, before her emotions flew too much higher and her inevitable fall from grace hit any harder. After the torment he'd put her through, surely Devlin owed her that much.

Not that she gave a hollow hoot about Devlin Stone now. From her seat, Eden glanced over the leather-bound menu while keeping an eye on the situation outside. His jacket flicked back, hands low on lean hips, Devlin spoke with the police officers, sometimes with a dark expression that made him look formidable, at others smiling as if he were catching up with old friends.

Devlin could charm the moon down from the sky.

Twenty minutes and two lime and sodas later, the police car pulled away. Eden had finished typing a message in her PDA—a reminder to check all her insurances were up to date—when her handsome ex walked in.

Anyone else might've looked dishevelled, but Devlin appeared only cool and controlled as he stopped at the desk, straightened his gold cufflinks, and ran an assessing eye over the room. Any spikes in his raven's-wing hair were stylish and deliberate. His lidded gaze was the same intense twilight blue she remembered. How she'd melted whenever those eyes had smiled at her—she'd felt so alive and adored.

And when they'd parted…

Setting her jaw, she reached for her cold glass.

Well, when they'd parted, she'd picked up the pieces and had never looked back.

After a directive tip of the maître d's head, Devlin wove between the tables. The flanking walls warped and shrank until he stood before her, a human tower, in more ways than one.

His features were both classically balanced yet hauntingly unique—a high forehead denoting intelligence, long straight nose suggesting inherent pride, squared-off jaw showing more than a hint of a sexy afternoon shadow. The word *beautiful* sprang to mind, in a mesmerising, purely masculine sense. His aura of strength and authority was so tangible, the female heads angled this way weren't likely to resume normal viewing any time soon.

Clearly Devlin Stone was dangerous.

Hell, that was half the attraction.

'Eden. Good to see you.'

Eden's nerve-endings reached out and purred at the familiar cadence of his rumbling low voice. Although her heart hammered against her ribs, she managed an unaffected smile.

'Hello, Devlin.'

'Sorry to keep you.' He retracted his chair. 'I was held up.'

Held up was right. Seemed women were still losing their minds over Devlin Stone—*literally*. The lesser part of her wanted to know the details—curiosity was, after all, a universal emotion. But Eden took the safer option: aloof good manners.

'That looked like quite an ordeal. I'm surprised the media didn't show up.'

His lip curling, Devlin shucked out of his jacket.

Well, well. Seemed he still disliked the paparazzi. Odd, when his brother seemed so fond of their attention.

'If you'd rather make this another time,' she offered. 'Tomorrow, perhaps—'

'Frankly, after that episode, I'm looking forward to unwinding with some pleasant company.' Above the tug of a lazy grin, his twilight gaze darkened. 'I'm glad you called.'

She felt her eyes widen as her insides squeezed and looped.

Hadn't he listened when she'd called yesterday? This meeting was *not* about them. 'Them' was dead and buried. No curtain call. No for old time's sake. He could work his charm all he liked, but she wasn't that naïve bright-eyed young thing any more. She wasn't here to flirt.

Devlin tipped his deeply cleft chin, beckoning a waiter who hurried over. 'Do you have Louis Roederer Cristal?'

The shorter man's eyes rounded in respect. 'We do indeed, sir.'

'Excellent. Chilled glasses, please.'

As Devlin surrendered his jacket for the cloakroom, Eden nibbled her lip. Exactly how much cloth did a tailor need to accommodate a set of shoulders like that?

'At last.' Devlin folded into his chair, clasped his big bronzed hands on the table and leant forward. 'I'm all yours.'

Her grin was wry.

As if.

'I appreciate your time, Devlin. I'd hoped we could discuss—' Cutting herself off, she frowned and touched her cheek. He was staring. 'Is something on my face?'

'On your lip.' He reached then stopped, his all-too-kissable mouth slanted at an amiable angle. 'May I?'

Eden's cheeks burned. Worse, so too did the tips of her breasts. She wanted to tell him to keep his hands to himself. But he'd already leaned over two sets of silverware…his thumb was already grazing the sensitive sweep of her lip…his hot fingers were already cupping her jaw…

And suddenly she was transported back to that fairy-tale summer long ago. She could hear his deep-throated laugh and her shrieks as they bumped around Luna Park's ghost-train tracks. She could feel the butterflies brushing her tummy the first time his warm giving mouth had tasted her in his bed. Three lost years faded and melted into now…

Then his hand drew away and her eyelids drifted open. The tinkling of cutlery and aroma of sautéed greens then chocolate soufflé hauled her back the rest of the way.

'Lime pulp,' he explained, nodding at the slice wedged

on her glass before gesturing for her to continue. 'You were saying?'

I was saying something?

She set two fingers against her giddy forehead.

Sabrina. Nathan Stone. Heartache.

Oh. yes.

Although she cleared her throat, her voice sounded tellingly deep. 'I wanted to talk to you about our siblings' situation.'

'You mean the fact they're dating?' Sexy creases—not quite brackets, not quite dimples—cut either side of his mouth. 'Have you seen them together?'

'Nathan's collected Sabrina from the lobby of our apartment a few times, but…no, she hasn't brought him up to meet me.'

No doubt Sabrina was worried about big sister's reaction. Sabrina knew all about Eden's ill-fated affair with Devlin. She'd listened to her lectures on staying away from heartless 'love 'em and leave 'em' types, the Stone brothers a classic case in point.

As though recalling something both wistful and amusing, Devlin chuckled and sat back. 'From what I can gather, they're hopelessly in love. I've never seen Nate like this before.'

'They've only been dating for six weeks,' she pointed out.

'I suppose,' he agreed. 'How long did we date? Fourteen, fifteen weeks?'

A hot chill dropped through her centre. *Sixteen weeks, two days, eleven hours,* if he really wanted to know. Long enough for Devlin to fall *out* of love rather than into it.

She fastened her hands together on the tabletop, her knuckles turning as white as the centrepiece roses. 'Can we please keep on track? We're talking about my sister—an impressionable girl in her final important year of university, spending time with a man who is best known for his rave parties on Mykonos.'

'*One* rave party.' His rumbling voice held a reproving note. 'And that was a year ago.'

'And twelve months is *such* a long time.'

'People mature.'

'Not everyone.' When his brow furrowed, she exhaled heavily. 'I didn't come here to insult you, Devlin.'

'Of course not.' His gaze gleamed with unadorned mischief. 'I'd hoped it might be to confess that you'd missed me.'

Her heartbeat skipped and she coughed out a bitter laugh. He was incorrigible. Conceited. And so frighteningly close to irresistible…

She knotted her arms over her chest and studied him through narrowed eyes. 'You really are an arrogant son of a—'

'And you're just as gorgeous as I remember.'

His gaze brushed her face, as intimate and thrilling as a lover's touch. Needing to make believe the flames licking her belly were shards of ice, she sat further back in the Glastonbury chair and crossed her legs. 'Are you going to help me or not?'

One big shoulder rolled up, then down. 'I'm not sure I know what you want.'

Fine. She'd spell it out. 'I want you to speak with your brother. Tell him to back off and leave Sabrina alone. She's delicate, Devlin. Easily hurt.' The couple at the next table slid over an enquiring glance. Reminded of their public setting, Eden tipped forward and dropped her voice. 'If this goes on any longer, she'll be shattered when Nathan ends their affair.'

'Who says he'll end it?'

She deadpanned back, 'How about the scores of heart-broken souls he's loved then left before now?'

Devlin held her gaze for a long considering moment as a muscle in his jaw popped. 'Admittedly Nate's had a few girlfriends—'

'More than a few,' she muttered.

'—but you're forgetting one thing. My brother is an adult. And your sister, I gather, is over twenty-one.'

'Barely.'

'We have no place interfering in their affairs.'

'That's easy for *you* to say. It's not your flesh and blood who'll spend months crying into her pillow every night—'

When his eyes flashed with interest, her cheeks caught light and she pressed her lips together. Way too much information.

Reaffirming the goal in her mind—to save her sister suffering the same pain she'd endured at the hands of a Stone—Eden tried again. 'I'm asking for your help.'

His pupils dilated until the deepest blue of his eyes became black. 'They're not kids, Eden. It's none of our business. It's nobody's business but theirs.'

At the implacable set of his jaw, she held her breath but couldn't stop the energy and hope seeping from her body.

So, that was that. She should've known this was useless. *Worse* than useless. Devlin Stone lived for two things: his next adventure and his next seduction, in that order, which didn't leave room for the compassion she'd hoped to find.

He'd probably instructed little brother more than once on the moves required to lay off a girl without accepting any blame. How dense to believe she might be able to talk to him. Worse, she'd put herself in this vulnerable position. He'd sent out the vibes, baiting her, testing her.

Tears born of frustration prickled the backs of her eyes.

She'd sooner scale the Harbour Bridge in a hailstorm than succumb to Devlin Stone's magnetism again.

'I'm sorry for wasting your time.' She pushed up on rubbery legs and calmly collected her purse. 'But I'm sure I'll feel sorrier for Sabrina.'

Devlin acknowledged and immediately dismissed the overwhelming urge to grab Eden's arm and haul her right back. She'd wanted to meet. He was here to talk. Yet ten minutes into their reunion he was watching the most exquisitely infuriating woman he'd ever known walk out on him.

Again!

Eden wanted him to step into the middle of his brother's affairs. Tell Nate who he should or should not see. She chose to ignore the fact that Nate and Sabrina were adults, old enough to make up their own minds, whether she approved or not. She might be slightly built, but Eden Foley entertained an Amazonian mentality.

She liked to be in control.

The waiter appeared and poured the champagne. Devlin sipped, barely tasting the fruity bubbles. His thoughts were stuck on the determined set of Eden's shoulders, the defiant passion in her apple-green eyes...

His gut muscles clenched and his line of vision darted to the restaurant's glass frontage at the same time Eden came into view. She looked edible in that cream-and-black dress, her chin and arm lifted high as she hailed a passing cab. That yellow didn't stop, but another would roll by soon enough. In a few minutes she'd be out of his life.

Again.

He ran a finger around his inside collar then, growling, pushed aside the crystal flute and strode towards the exit, tossing enough cash on the desk as he passed.

Damnation, what was it about that woman? Her exceptional figure? Her sharp wit? That glossy honey-blonde hair?

Yes, yes and yes.

And something more. Something that gnawed at him whenever he woke and wondered in the still dead of night.

The remnants of a need to tame her?

He claimed his jacket from the brunette at the counter, threw it over a shoulder and headed out.

No, submission wasn't the prize. He'd never had the desire to tame any woman—only enjoy them. Spoil them. In his younger day the world had seemed full of alluring possibilities. Then his offshore oil and gas support company had taken off *and* he'd met Eden—a woman who possessed the contradictory seeds of both natural innocence and darkest temptation…a curious and, as it'd turned out, addictive combination.

Yesterday, when his secretary had said Eden Foley was on the line, his palm was damp by the time he'd picked up. He'd accepted Eden's invitation and had spent a restless night anticipating their coming encounter. When he'd jumped out of that cab earlier, God help him, he'd wanted to shirk civic duty and bypass that whacko hitting a home run on some poor bastard's car. Her *husband's* car, so that officer had said.

Stepping outside, Devlin sucked in a cleansing breath while thunder grumbled overhead.

Marriage. What a racket.

He spied Eden on the footpath, raised on the balls of her sexy black heels, flagging another cab. He scrubbed his jaw and scrubbed it again.

Time to face facts. The memory of that woman still had him by the horns and that was far from acceptable. But there was a remedy, one simple answer to one simple question. When he had that, he could put that nameless ghost to bed and Eden Foley out of his mind for good.

He stopped beside her and, hands in his pockets, perused the steady stream of traffic as a cooling breeze on a muggy day combed through his hair. 'It's busy for a Saturday.'

She stiffened at his voice but didn't meet his eyes. 'Less busy than earlier. I see they've towed your car away.'

He did a double take. 'You mean the crippled BMW?' He shook his head. 'Nice automobile, but not mine.'

She slumped on a weary sigh. 'Devlin, I saw the woman pummel the bonnet, saw you swing around the back and lift the bat right out of her hands. Of course it was your car.'

Guess it could've looked that way, but, 'I happened to be in the right place at the wrong time. There were kids on the path. Someone had to stop her. I only wish I'd known a police car was cruising by. Would've saved me a pile of trouble.'

Her expression changed, from annoyed disinterest to stilted comprehension. 'Y-you didn't know her?'

'You think I have some crazy cousin in the family?'

'Not a cousin…'

The penny dropped along with his jaw. 'Oh, Eden, no. You didn't think that woman and I were an *item*?'

'All the pieces seemed to fit.' The confusion in her eyes cleared. 'I should've guessed the other explanation.'

As her words trailed, a cold splash landed on his nose

at the same time the earthy scent of rain hitting hot cement rose off the pavement. He shot a glance at the churning grey sky. A heartbeat later, the heavens opened up.

Eden yelped, hunching over as icy needles pelted down. Thinking for them both, he gathered her close, threw his jacket over their heads for protection and scooted towards a shallow alcove set in the building's façade. Tight but room enough for two.

As he shook out his jacket she let go a sorrowful wail. 'I'm soaked!'

'It's not fatal. You'll dry.'

'Not before this outfit is ready for the trash. It's new-season fine wool blend. Strictly dry-clean only. It was going in my window Monday morning. Hundreds of dollars, and orders besides, down the drain.'

He'd known she owned a boutique in town. Given the snippets he'd gleaned from ladies at recent black-tie functions, Temptations had built a reputation for its classy inventory. And that dress was a knockout, soaked through or not. Tasteful yet sexy, a far cry from the hip-riding jeans she'd worn—and he'd loved—when they'd first met.

Beside him, she trembled, hugged herself, and his arm instinctively went out to warm her. 'You're cold.'

She shied away. 'I shake when I'm mad.'

He relaxed and hid a grin. He remembered. She shook at other times too.

'Things could be worse.'

Pressing herself to the wall, she recrossed her arms and thinned her lips.

He laughed. 'Oh, come on. When did you become such a sourpuss?'

'Since your brother began dating my sister. And before

you start, you've made your stand on that subject very clear. I'd rather not go there again.'

She was right. There was nothing more to discuss on that issue. Nate could work out his own affairs. However, confined as they were because of this downpour, now seemed an ideal time to touch on that other long overdue matter.

Devlin propped his shoulders against the wall, jacket draped over his crossed arms, and gazed casually out at the veil of teeming rain.

'Eden, why didn't you return my calls?'

'You called back yesterday?'

He turned his head to stare down her Miss Innocent look. 'I mean three years ago.'

Her green eyes cooled and she shook her head slowly. 'I shouldn't be surprised.'

He cocked a brow. 'That's not much of an answer.'

'Here's the rest. I shouldn't be surprised by your unwillingness to take responsibility.'

Her grave tone was meant to bite. Instead her indignation shot a searing arrow straight to his groin. Damn, she was cute when she was mad. Didn't mean he had a clue what she was on about.

'So I'm irresponsible now?'

'I know it'll come as a shock,' she stated, 'but not all women are prepared to hang around to watch the final curtain fall.'

He pushed off the wall.

Okay. He had a slippery handle on this now. He enunciated each word carefully so no one got confused. 'You're saying you dumped *me* before I could dump *you*?'

'You left for the UK that last morning without saying goodbye.'

Correct. 'You were asleep. I didn't want to wake you.'

'You didn't call when you landed.'

His brow lowered. 'I didn't realise I had to check in.'

'You took another flight and boarded a ship that capsized in the freezing waters of the North Sea.'

He held off from rolling his eyes.

Here it comes.

Before he and Eden had even met, he'd organised with an industry colleague to check out their operations west of the Shetland Islands. The vessel—an anchor-handling tug—had been commissioned to recover and relocate the eighteen-tonne anchors of an oil drilling rig. A manoeuvre, preparing for a hard turn to starboard to increase stability, had resulted in the winch chain snapping across the deck and around to the port side. The tug had been pulled over. Human, technical or design error…the investigation into the accident had come back inconclusive.

He rubbed the corner of one eye. 'Look, I understand you were worried. I spoke with you as soon as I could.'

Her stony mask broke. 'Devlin, the accident was on the news! I couldn't get hold of anyone who knew anything. I was worried out of my *mind.* And when I finally spoke to you, you as good as told me I was overreacting.'

Her heart was there, shining from the depths of her eyes and, irrespective of the fact he'd done nothing wrong, his chest squeezed around a fist full of guilt.

'Nobody died,' he reminded her, recalling the blaze of cameras when he'd finally got to shore after the accident. 'I was fine.'

'Just like you're fine when you fly your ultra-light planes?'

His nostrils flared. 'It's a hobby I enjoy.'

'Just like you'll be fine when you finally climb Eiger's deadly North Face?'

'I was kidding about that.' Until he had more Alps experience, anyway.

'Like you're fine when you, you—' she flung a frustrated arm towards the rain '—when you wrestle with maniacs in the *street*.'

His groan was half growl. 'Eden, please—'

'You don't shy away from danger, risk, adventure,' she went on. 'While I, on the other hand, am a big fan of silly things like safety, security, predictability. It was nice while it lasted, Devlin. *Really* nice. But let's face it…' Her green eyes glistened and her voice lowered. 'I wasn't exciting enough for you. We'd drifted apart even before you left for Scotland that day.'

The pain and regret in her eyes faded before resignation dropped like a mask over her face once again. She dragged in a breath and, as if they'd been discussing the weather, inspected the sky. 'I think the rain's easing off.'

His arms knotted over his wet thumping chest.

Not so quick.

'We're not finished.'

'We were finished three years ago.'

He measured her with his eyes. She appeared reconciled, but he saw the way her chest rose and fell beneath that designer dress, the way she bit her lip as she angled her face away.

Five days a week he sat behind a desk, organising specialist crews to tackle hands-on tasks associated with offshore rigs. So what was wrong with getting outdoors and amongst it himself when he could? He wanted to *live* life, damn it, not stand back and watch the world go by.

Why couldn't Eden get that about him? They'd always been so in tune in other ways. They'd laughed at the same things, liked the same food, enjoyed the same music. They were explosive in the bedroom. And, as far as being distant before he'd left was concerned…

He ground his back teeth and rearranged his feet.

There was that one episode…the morning when she'd sat parked at the end of his kitchen counter, dressed in his Raiders tee, pink fluffy slippers on her feet, flipping through a jewellery catalogue. She'd looked up, wound some golden hair behind an ear and murmured, 'Hey, babe, whatchoo doing?' Then she'd sent over an angelic wanna-take-me-back-to-bed smile. If she'd been checking out necklaces or earrings in that catalogue, broaches or bracelets or charms—

But *diamond rings…*?

He winced at the same time a phone buzzed. Eden collected her cell, then the BlackBerry on his belt sounded.

While he listened to his voicemail, Eden read a text then carefully put her phone away. Her dazed look must have matched his own.

'That text was from Sabrina,' she murmured. 'She wants me to meet her.'

'Mine was from Nate. He said the same.'

She hunted down his gaze. 'To meet him at a city hotel?'

She named the place and he nodded. 'Nate said he had some important news to share.'

She visibly paled. 'You don't think they've done something foolish?'

'Like get married?'

'Like get *pregnant*.'

Devlin's surroundings seemed to darken, tunnel, then caved in.

Given the brothers' family history, a quickie wedding didn't seem likely. Marriage certainly didn't feature anywhere near the top of Devlin's personal agenda. However, if Nate *had* exchanged vows after six short weeks, the move was far from fatal. If *sweet* turned to *sour*, there was always divorce, an option his parents should've considered before pushing ahead and having two kids.

But if Nate had got this girl pregnant—if Sabrina was carrying Nate's baby—*that* was sacrosanct. As far as responsibility and duty went, there was no middle ground where a child was concerned. A man had to be there for his own flesh and blood. Nate would appreciate that fact.

Again employing his jacket as a makeshift umbrella, Devlin dashed out into the lashing rain and lunged off the pavement to stop a slow-moving cab. As the yellow pulled up, he signalled Eden over. She bolted towards him, kicking up water as her heels smacked the puddles.

But when he opened the passenger door, she hesitated, her hair glued to her scalp, lashes heavy with rain, that dress shrinking before his appreciative eyes.

'Maybe I should get the next one,' he heard her say over the torrent.

Now they were out of that cubbyhole they'd sheltered in, she didn't want to be close to him? She didn't trust him. Or was it that Eden didn't trust herself?

Done with the tippy-toe show, he flung his jacket into the back of the cab then stood tall, hands low on hips, legs braced apart. 'I have a better idea. Why don't we just get this over with?'

Her brow furrowed as rain sped down her cheeks and curled around her chin. 'I don't know what you mean.'

'I think you do.'

She scoffed. 'You think you know everything.'

'Let's say I'm working on it.'

He stepped into the space separating them, drew her against his chest and, before she could object, he kissed her—deeply, passionately and without a hint of mercy. And, at long last, he had his answer.

Because Eden stiffened, shivered.

Then she kissed him back.

CHAPTER TWO

THE heady sensation of Devlin's mouth moving over hers had the same effect as a defibrillator igniting a stalled heartbeat.

Electric. Life-giving.

Essential for survival.

Somewhere in the back of her whirling mind, Eden knew they stood on a pavement, in the middle of a downpour, smack-dab in the centre of Sydney. But, like a billowing mist, the memory of everything that had come before grew hazy. All she knew—all she *wanted* to know—was the natural high humming through her blood, the jet of flames leaping from his body directly to hers.

As his big hot hands wove along her shoulders to cup her wet face, her mind's eye saw his broad shoulders looming over her. Helpless to fight against the tide, she gripped his soaked shirt as burgeoning desire thickened and ached in her throat.

His palm scooped around her nape and gently tugged her hair until her mouth opened more. He kissed deeper, stepped closer. When the solid ridge trapped inside his trousers pressed against her belly, her pelvic floor pulsed with burning want. Three years without his caress...all those nights spent alone...

Way too good.

Way too long.

His touch slid down to settle firmly on the small of her back as the edge of his tongue swept around hers and Eden melted more. But when a satisfied growl rumbled in his chest, a sliver of doubt feathered up her spine and a single word whispered through the fog. She didn't want to listen, but she heard it anyway.

Danger...

Her fingers dug into his hard chest one last time before she groaned and wrenched herself free. Once she'd been in love with Devlin, but at least she'd walked away with her dignity intact.

Where was her dignity now?

Out of breath, she dragged the drenched hair off her face and glanced around. Most people were either dashing from the downpour or had already found shelter. No one seemed concerned with the demonstrative couple kissing in the rain. That didn't mean Eden wasn't horrified, at herself more so than Devlin.

He didn't want to own up to the fact that he'd become restless of her company three years ago. He certainly wouldn't acknowledge why he'd kissed her now. This very public embrace was no more than a display. By subduing her here, he got to reclaim a portion of the power he'd lost when she'd ended the affair.

Devlin abhorred losing, even someone he'd grown tired of.

'I'll take this cab with you,' she said in a breathy voice. 'But if you touch me again—even one finger—'

His smiling eyes simmered more. 'Yes, Eden?'

'When I meet your brother, I'll do what I wanted to do

from the start.' Her throat convulsed and she paused to swallow. 'Tell him exactly what I think.'

Devlin's penetrating gaze didn't change. He wasn't listening. Was it imagination that he'd moved close again?

With her body still burning for him, she bunched a hand by her side.

Damn it, he needed to back off—*now*!

She grabbed at the only weapon that flew to mind. 'Devlin, if you try to kiss me again I swear I'll not only tell your brother he's a pleasure-seeking brat, a two-bit playboy turned cradle snatcher, but I'll do it in front of as many cameras as I can. If I'm loud enough, it might even stir up a few paternity suits.'

Devlin's head kicked back. His dark lashes, clumped with water, blinked twice. 'You'd purposely bring reporters into their relationship? You'd hurt your sister like that?'

'You have it wrong. I don't want to see anyone hurt, least of all my sister.'

Swinging around him, she scooted inside the cab, finally out of the rain. Following, he closed the door with a heavy *smack*. He grumbled the address to the driver, a friendly man, who chatted about the shocking weather and the monsoon season in India, while she and Devlin each glared out of their respective windows.

She didn't argue when Devlin settled the fare; rather she marched ahead into the hotel's opulent soaring foyer. He caught up and when they reached the marble-and-gold-rimmed reception desk, soaked to the bone, she let Devlin do the talking. She was still shaking like a half-formed jelly inside.

Although she was less than proud of herself, thank God her bluff had worked. While she doubted Nathan Stone worried a jot over his bad-boy image, Devlin loathed the press. Couple that dislike with his highly protective streak and threatening Nathan's interests had seemed the only surefire way to have Devlin back off.

On a basic level, Eden couldn't cheapen Devlin's commitment to his brother. She, too, was fiercely protective of those she loved. There wasn't a thing she wouldn't do to keep Sabrina safe.

At the reception counter, Devlin drove that hand through his slick pitch-black hair as a young woman sped up.

The ponytailed blonde in a crisp olive-green uniform seemed eager to please. 'How can I help, sir?'

'Put me through to Nathan Stone's room.'

Miss Ponytail's hazel eyes rounded. 'Are you Devlin Stone?' When he nodded, she handed over a key card. 'The other Mr Stone asked that I give you access to his penthouse suite.'

Inspecting the card, he muttered a curt thanks and Eden followed his long purposeful strides to the lifts. Riding to the top floor, Devlin broke their suffocating silence.

'Whatever's said, you won't make a scene,' he announced in a lethal tone.

'I'll be as cool as a cucumber,' she replied, feeling anything but. 'If they're married or pregnant—' she shuddered but accepted the unacceptable '—I'll be nothing but supportive.'

His tone was sardonic. 'But you'll be less than thrilled.'

She straightened the drenched line of her dress. 'I want my sister to be happy. I'm far from convinced Nathan Stone can do that.'

'You're condemning him without a trial.'

'The media have done a thorough job of that already.'

His growl resonated off the mirrored lift walls. 'The paparazzi dig for sensationalism and if they can't find any, they make it up. A wealthy young man is a prime target—' his voice deepened '—as you've already made clear.'

The lift door whirred open and she walked out ahead of him, lamenting, 'Oh, the burdens of the rich and famous.'

Devlin might have dematerialised and reappeared, he whipped around and cut her off so quickly. His dark eyes glared down at her, more thunderous than this afternoon's sky.

'You're angry with me for kissing you,' he said with frightening control. 'I can't regret doing it. I won't deny I want to do it again, but I suspect that's due more to mindless adrenaline than any charm on your part. But let me assure you, I won't touch you again. I have my answer, so you can drop the snarky attitude.'

With her blood draining to her toes, she could only utter, 'Your answer?'

His stormy eyes roamed her face before he yanked loose the knot at his throat and, after a tense moment, stepped aside.

'You convinced me, okay? I'd always wondered. But, however it happened, whatever lay behind it, I should've been fine with you walking away. Case closed.'

The crimson carpet tilted beneath her feet. If he hadn't already walked on ahead she might've grabbed his arm for support. First he'd been charming, then seductive, and now fierce followed by dismissive. This latest reaction suited her fine. Her performance had turned him off. He wouldn't touch her again, even if he wanted to.

Shoring up her inner strength, she willed the light-headed tingles away and moved forward.

Devlin rang the bell, ripped free his loosened tie, then

rapped his knuckles on the wood. With no answer, he swiped his card and pushed in the door. 'Nate, you here?'

Eden followed him inside.

With the air-con cooler in the suite, she was reminded of her saturated clothing. Her teeth began to chatter as she searched around the sumptuous furnishings, a foreground to elaborate scarlet and beige window dressings.

'Sabrina. Honey, it's Eden. Where are you?'

Devlin scanned the room then strode to a polished timber table and swept up a note slanted against a tall vase of lilies. When his hand lowered and his face hardened, Eden hurried over.

'What is it?' she prodded. 'What does it say?'

'They needed to go out.' He stuffed his tie in a pocket. 'They'll be back by five.'

Eden held onto the table edge. 'That's two hours away. What are we supposed to do until then?'

'Hopefully not kill each other.'

They both must've had the same thought—to see if there was any possibility that their siblings might return earlier. She dug out her cell phone as Devlin dived on his. They dialled and, after a few seconds, both rang off.

'Sabrina's phone isn't on,' she said.

'Neither is Nate's.'

'We could meet back here at five?'

He tossed his phone and wallet on the table then, with a casual fluid gait, moved towards some adjoining double doors. 'You go ahead.'

She took an automatic step forward, then back. 'Where are you going?'

'To have a warm shower, organise my clothes to be express cleaned, then wait for my brother to arrive.'

Eden flinched. Sabrina and Nathan might arrive *before* five. She needed to be here to support her sister. What if Sabrina were pregnant and Nathan's reaction to the news hadn't been all honey and roses? What if Nathan had asked her to marry him and Sabrina wanted her big sister's blessing?

Or advice?

Spending more time alone with Devlin was anathema to her personal ethos—safety first. But what option did she have?

Leaning on the table, she slipped off a shoe and glanced dejectedly around. 'This is a big place. We don't exactly need to bump into each other.'

With his frame filling the doorway, Devlin rotated to face her, his smile a combination of blatant sex appeal and ice. 'Rest assured, Eden, I'll make a point of it.'

The bedroom door slapped shut.

Devlin strode into the enormous bedroom suite and slashed both sets of fingers through his hair.

Damnation! That woman could get under his skin—even when he knew darn well her threat had been an empty one.

She might be determined and dedicated—she wanted what she thought was best for her sister—but Eden wasn't without scruples. Whether or not she bought into the beat-ups that depicted Nate as some kind of amoral hotshot playboy, she wouldn't call the media hounds out simply because big brother had skipped the double talk and gone straight to the heart of the matter. Or was Eden forgetting that she'd kissed him back?

Cocking a brow, he released a cufflink.

Boy, had she kissed him back.

Which finally gave him closure on his long-unanswered question.

Eden was still attracted to him—at least physically, he amended, crossing the room. She hadn't returned his calls three years ago, but not because she hadn't wanted to. She'd seen the writing on the wall and had decided to walk before he'd done the walking.

Unbuttoning his shirt, Devlin sank onto the edge of the king-sized bed and heeled off his sodden shoes.

She'd been wrong. He hadn't been about to cut her off—even if he could admit now that, yes, perhaps he had contemplated cooling things a degree or two. After diamond rings, a woman wanted wedding bands. He hadn't been ready for a stroll down the aisle.

His position hadn't changed.

His father had married too soon and had never accepted his family-man status. As a tyke, Devlin hadn't understood why his dad stayed late at the office every night. 'He's a busy man,' his mother would say gently when she tucked her little son in. 'Go to sleep now. You'll see Daddy tomorrow.'

Devlin had thought his mother the most beautiful woman on earth. Who could blame his father for jumping the gun and sweeping her off to the chapel? A quietly spoken angel with a warm loving smile who, as far as a young Devlin could tell, existed in a separate world he was rarely able to penetrate.

When Nate had come along, the boys had kept each other company while their mother had spent more and more time alone, usually in a darkened room. 'I have a migraine,' she'd tell the nanny. 'Make sure the boys do their homework before going to bed.'

Headaches? Or had his mother simply hidden away from

more companionless days while her husband's days—and nights—were splashed across the tabloid pages?

Grunting, Devlin discarded his shirt.

His father had not only married too soon, his father shouldn't have married at all.

But, the past was past, he reminded himself, grabbing the side table's receiver and punching in Housekeeping's number. He and Nate hadn't even discussed their less-than-perfect upbringing, although his brother must've felt the same unhealthy undercurrent in the family dynamics. That was why, if this afternoon's meeting was in honour of a quickie marriage, the maths didn't add up. Or was it as Eden suspected and Nate had gone and got his girl pregnant?

Having organised for his clothes to be collected, Devlin stripped off his trousers and stood face up under a strong steamy shower for five revitalising minutes. He was lashing a towel around his hips when the doorbell sounded. Shoving his wet clothes into an in-house laundry bag, he strode out of the bedroom and headed for the door.

'Hold up!'

At Eden's voice, he wheeled back and drank in the pulse-racing sight—diminutive Eden draped in a thick oversized courtesy robe, a white towel turbaned on her head, Leaning-Tower-of-Pisa style. What he could see of her bare legs revealed tanned silky-smooth skin. Each perfect toenail was painted a provocative red. Her heart-shaped face was scrubbed clean of make-up and as his gaze licked her lips—pink and full—he swore he tasted the raw honey he'd sampled earlier in the rain.

Wild and wickedly sweet.

Bare feet sinking into the plush white carpet, she presented her own laundry bag.

'Here's mine.' She waited for his response, then slanted her head, catching the toppling turban. 'Devlin, are you going to get the door?'

He couldn't tear his gaze from her mouth. And more than the mere *sight* of her sparked his imagination. The way she smelled didn't help one bit—fresh…natural.

Good enough to eat.

Devlin flexed his free hand and, suppressing a groan, swung open the door.

They needed to get their clothes back—*fast*.

A lanky bell-hop took both bags. 'When do you want these back, sir?'

'Yesterday,' Devlin growled under an overload of frustration, 'and hurry up.'

The boy's eyes popped. 'I'm, er, not sure that…'

'He means as soon as humanly possible,' Eden explained amenably.

The boy's mouth twitched on a nervous smile. 'Within the hour, okay, ma'am?'

She reached to close the door. 'That'll be fine.'

Alone again, they eyed each other as white-hot energy buzzed and skipped between them. Compressing her lips into a determined line, Eden wrapped the bulky robe more firmly over her breasts. As if that weren't enough, she yanked on her robe's sash.

'Pull that sash any tighter,' he said, forcing himself to stroll away, 'and you'll cut off your circulation.'

She made an indignant sound. 'At least I'm not parading around, showing off my bare chest.'

Folding his arms—accentuating that chest—he rotated back. 'My body bothers you?'

Best he could remember her favourite game had been

trailing the tip of her tongue down his centre, reaching the toe-curling point where she'd run a slow circle around his navel. Then she'd climb again, drawing a wet line around each of his nipples while raking her nails down his shoulders and sides. Driven out of his mind, he would finally roll and pin her beneath him. Then it was his turn to play.

Perhaps Eden had read his eyes—had guessed his smouldering thoughts—because her cheeks pinked up more and she shrank away.

'You could stride around buck naked,' she declared, pulling that sash again, 'and it wouldn't make a scrap of difference to me.'

He coughed a dry laugh. 'You're so certain.'

She strolled towards the enormous semi-circular lounge. 'I won't dignify that with a response.'

'Then maybe we should put your assertion to the test.'

She swung back, fear and dreaded desire shining in her eyes. 'I warned you, Devlin. Don't try to rattle me.'

One side of his mouth curved up. 'Rattle wasn't the word that sprang to mind.'

After sauntering past her, he swallowed a self-admonishing groan and clamped his eyes shut.

She was doing it *again*. Getting under his skin. Making him want her without even trying. But, no matter how strong the tug, sex—and anything remotely connected to the act—was off the table. They'd failed once. Neither of them needed to repeat history. Diamond rings and Devlin Stone were a no-go zone. Unfortunately they were stuck here together, alone, until Nate and his girlfriend arrived.

Halfway back to the bedroom, Devlin's gait faltered.

Important news…*big* news…

What if this announcement wasn't marriage or a baby, but

rather an engagement? There'd be wedding rehearsals, the ceremony, speeches and playing happy families. Which meant he and Eden would need to shelve their sparring gloves for an extended period, even if the truce was all show.

This short stint of forced proximity might only be the beginning.

Rubbing the ache at his temple, he angled back.

'Eden, I have a proposition.'

She stood by the floor-to-ceiling window, arms ravelled tightly before her, glaring out at Sydney's spectacular city-scape, the sleek arched line of the Harbour Bridge to the left.

'If it involves playing strip poker until the kids arrive,' she said to the view, 'count me out.'

'Strip poker hadn't crossed my mind.' Although now she'd mentioned it...

He smothered the idea and cleared his throat. 'I want to put something to you, something that'll be in the best interests of your sister and my brother.'

Her wary gaze slid over. 'Go on.'

'Whatever's coming, we need to be supportive.'

After a thoughtful moment, she sighed and dragged the towel turban from her head. 'Agreed.'

'We won't seem too supportive if we can't speak to each other without reaching for the closest poison-tipped spear.'

Her teeth worried her plump lower lip before she absently finger-combed her wet hair and draped the towel over a chair. 'I guess not.'

'Let's at least try to get along for Sabrina and Nate's sake. Surely it's not that difficult. We're mature adults.'

'Well, *I* am.' She grimaced. 'Sorry. You're right. This won't do.' She sent a brave smile. 'I'm more than happy to put our differences aside and play nice for their sake.'

Exhaling, he put out his hand. 'Deal?'

She stepped forward. 'Deal.'

He took her hand. The sizzle, crackling up the cords of his arm, was the same high-voltage zap he'd enjoyed earlier when his mouth had claimed hers. When the charge reached his shoulder, crackle turned to burn, racing through his system and hitting him hard where his blood already blazed and beat.

Her eyes flashed, her breath audibly hitched. Their fingers were as good as fused, but if he didn't let go soon they'd both be in big trouble.

If he didn't know there'd be lasting repercussions—if he didn't know he'd regret it—he'd make love to Eden in a heartbeat. But, even if by some miracle she agreed to succumb and satisfy this rabid sexual urge, becoming involved again wasn't worth the drama.

Was it?

An unconscious primal impulse tightened his grip before he pried his fingers from hers. He needed to put them somewhere; his hands went to his pockets.

He shot a glance south.

Right. He wasn't wearing trousers. More to the point, neither he nor Eden were wearing clothes. One towel, one robe, stood between him and a woman whose thrall, near or far, refused to cut him free.

Rubbing the back of his neck, he tossed a look around.

Man, he needed a drink.

Striding to the granite wet bar, he swung down a couple of wine glasses hanging from their overhead rack. 'Want a drink?'

His throat felt drier than the Simpson.

She replied, 'I really don't think that's such a good—'

His gaze shot to hers and she sucked back the retort at the same time her features softened with a convivial, almost understanding smile that said if he was fighting so hard to keep this platonic—friendly but impersonal—so would she.

'That would be nice, Devlin. Thank you.'

Opening the fridge, he reached for champagne. Then, remembering the unfinished Cristal, he uncorked and poured domestic Chardonnay instead. A lifetime ago, champagne had been *their* drink. Eden would drop a strawberry into her glass and when the bubbles were gone, she'd share her fruit—one bite for her, one bite for him. He would draw the flesh into his mouth, suck the nectar from her fingers, kiss the sweet juice from her lips…

Something wet dribbled onto his toes.

Jumping back, he swore aloud. Off with the fairies, he'd over-poured the second glass. Wine had puddled on the counter, was pooling on the floor.

Of all the stupid, careless—

Eden had swung around. 'What's wrong?'

He muttered something about losing his grip, then joined her again. He handed over her wine, careful not to let their fingers touch this time. Putting an effort into appreciating the vibrant harbour view, he brought his glass to his lips. 'The rain's stopped.'

Her finger drew a curve in the air. 'There's a rainbow.'

A far-reaching arc of red, violet and every colour in between bowed over the giant Opera House shells, touching the glistening harbour waters either side.

Nice.

'Did you know that the colours of a rainbow are a result of light refracted off of raindrops?' he said.

'That's such a clinical way of looking at—' She cut her

jibe short and rephrased. 'What I mean is, I'd always looked at rainbows in a magical rather than scientific light. It's good to get the other side.'

He grinned, then softly chuckled. She was trying so hard. Trying to do the best by her sister.

His gaze veered away from the sky—spent grey streaking westward to leave newly washed blue—and settled on the equally mesmerising sight beside him.

His heart fisted in his throat.

No contest. She was even more beautiful than he'd remembered.

His next words were unintentionally husky. 'So you believe in magic?'

Concentrating on the rainbow, she hesitated before her chin picked up. 'Sure. Why not?'

His gaze drank her in. 'Then you'd believe there's a pot of gold at every rainbow's end.'

Her brow pinched and her throat bobbed before she murmured so faintly he barely heard.

'I believed it once.'

CHAPTER THREE

HER cheeks caught light as a withering feeling fell through her middle.

Good one, Eden. Try to sound a little more wistful and pathetic next time.

But, rather than comment on her whimsy, thankfully Devlin only turned his attention back towards the colourful view.

Still, no one could deny the heady awareness throbbing between them. Hot, alive. But different this time. Different from when they touched. This was more a swift warm current swirling around them, washing up memories of what they'd once shared…what they'd let slip away…

Loosening the grip on her glass, Eden laughed at herself.

Good grief. Next thing she'd convince herself that Devlin had actually *loved* her once.

As if responding to her thought, Devlin downed the rest of his glass and walked away. 'It's warm in here.'

The room had felt icy when they'd first entered. Now…yes, it was warm and getting warmer, despite both their efforts to keep the temperature down. But great sex—even bone-melting, unforgettable sex—wasn't the answer.

So why did her gaze insist on trailing the broad expanse

of his back as he walked off…? Why did she imagine her mouth tracing the salty heat of his skin?

Dragging her gaze away—needing to douse the tingles chasing over her flesh—she gulped down half of her drink.

They'd tried arguing, being nice. Maybe it was time to put up a wall. Quit communication altogether. Get as far away from Devlin and his maleficent magnetism as this enormous penthouse suite would allow. That wouldn't be rude, merely smart.

After a harried search, her gaze landed on a glossy magazine. She passed a monstrous gilt mirror, a postmodernist sculpture of lovers embracing, and, at the far side of the room, swiped the heavy magazine off the coffee table. In the nick of time, she stopped from lowering into the damask couch. Too much opportunity there. Devlin might sit down beside her. Way too close for comfort.

She glanced towards the balcony.

Not in a robe.

One of the two bedrooms?

Oh, Lord, no.

Her gaze dropped.

The carpet certainly felt soft enough. She eased down onto the pile and, back against the sofa, crossed her ankles of her outstretched robe-covered legs then buried her nose in the magazine.

At the bar, Devlin topped up, but then set the glass aside.

'I'm starved,' he announced, as if he too had found the answer to their problem. 'Want something to eat?'

Although she'd lost her appetite, her stomach felt empty. She really ought to eat something.

She shrugged. 'I'll have a salad.'

After ordering, Devlin settled down for a few minutes

to do some work on his BlackBerry. When he was finished, he slid the phone back onto the polished table. In her peripheral vision, she saw him thatch his fingers behind his head. He stretched his washboard waist one way then the other before letting those impressive arms drop to his sides.

'You look engrossed,' he said.

She didn't look up. 'I always find fashion interesting.'

He wandered closer. 'When did you open your boutique?'

'The month after—' She caught herself. She didn't need to mention their break-up again. 'A couple of years ago now.' Three to be precise.

'So that dress-design course paid off?'

She gave a wry smile. Actually she'd earned an advanced diploma in fashion design and technology at East Sydney College.

'The business degree I'm doing part-time helps too,' she told him, 'as well as trips to Paris, Milan, New York.'

He let out a low whistle. 'You've been around.'

'If I want to compete with the top outlets, I need to.' Although boarding a plane was always a battle, especially long international flights. Bad turbulence could make her whimper. And seeing *Red Eye* hadn't helped her phobia one bit.

He piped up, 'I thought you were afraid of flying.'

Unlike ultra-light skylarking, 'Boarding airbuses is a necessary vocational risk.'

'Risks can pay off.'

She finally met his gaze. 'Risks can kill.'

In fact—

She dug her nose back into the Venetian spring fashion exclusive at the same time the doorbell rang.

Devlin set off. 'Food's here.'

She would have followed and, perhaps, pulled up a chair at the formal setting. But if they sat at the table, they might look into each other's eyes, maybe accidentally touch. She shivered and brought the magazine closer to her face.

Far wiser to stay put.

Still, over the top of the pages, she cased out those remarkable muscled limbs as he sauntered towards the door, each languid movement perfectly in tune with his casually commanding style. The instant he turned back, silver-domed plates balanced in each hand, she buried her gaze again.

When he lowered her meal to where she sat on the floor, she set her magazine down. Dome removed, her appetite bit at the colourful fig, apple and pecan-nut salad. The yoghurt aioli smelled delicious. She was hungrier than she'd thought.

Devlin positioned himself on the couch, but with his back against the far cushioned arm, long legs stretched out along the seat, a club sandwich and fries on his lap.

Eden held her breath.

Maybe she *should* have sat at the table. In this intimate corner of the room, with the natural light barely reaching them, this seating arrangement felt far too…opportunistic.

But he seemed to be behaving himself. Given he'd made the affable gesture to join her, but not too close, jumping up now to eat at the table alone would look noticeably rude and, hopefully, unnecessary.

After a few moments of mutual munching, Devlin sucked the salt and sour cream off his thumb and noted, 'That looks, uh, *healthy*.' He offered a chip. 'Want to try one of these?'

Her fork tapped her plate. 'I prefer natural ingredients.'

'Fries are natural too. Potato cooked in natural oil seasoned with natural salt. Three food groups, and I haven't even started on the sandwich.'

A smile played around her mouth. She'd missed his dry humour…the slight burr in his speech whenever he teased through a crooked grin.

Letting her guard down a little more, she stabbed at some blue-vein cheese. They had time for a lesson in nutrition.

'The calcium in dairy foods like cheese is terrific for healthy bones.'

His mouth twisted. 'Mouldy cheese and I don't get along.'

Fair enough. 'Fruit is great for glowing skin.' She held up a slice of apple. Then, remembering the champagne-infused fruit she used to feed him when they'd dated, she rethought the move.

But he'd already leaned forward to loosen the apple off her fork. 'Glowing skin, huh?' He flexed a brow. 'How can I resist?'

He popped the slice into his mouth and slid down from the couch onto the carpet alongside her. His plate settled on the floor to his left as he chewed, swallowed, then licked his lips.

'Nice.' He tipped his chin at her plate. 'And that?'

Although her stomach somersaulted and better judgement screamed to move away, she preferred to stay calm. She wasn't a baby. She could handle Devlin Stone. She'd got him to back off earlier, hadn't she? He knew she was serious. What was more, notwithstanding the chronic sexual pull, he didn't want to get involved any more than she did. He was merely trying to get along for the kids' sake.

She indicated the pecans. 'Nuts are protein rich. They're delicious mixed with cereal when you jump out of bed in the morning.'

'What if you don't want to jump out of bed? What if you want to take your time?'

She slid him an arch look. Was he being light or leading?

Looking offended, he pinned back his shoulders. 'What? I'm only saying that I enjoy a good long stretch in the morning.'

Feeling her breasts swell, she sidled a little away. She knew very well how much he enjoyed his *stretch* in the morning.

He drew up his legs and angled one tanned forearm over a bare knee while he started on his sandwich. When his towel marginally slid up his athletic thigh, a pulse fluttered in her throat and she swallowed hard.

How on earth was she supposed to eat now?

After a few automaton mouthfuls—trying to keep her mind and gaze off her companion—she announced, 'Delicious, but I'm full.'

He wiped his mouth on a napkin. 'Me too.' He leaned over to take more apple from her plate, then stopped to ask, 'Do you mind?'

She forced a smile that didn't betray how fast her heart was beating. 'Silly to let it go to waste.'

Drawing away, he took a bite from the slice. 'So, what's next on the agenda?'

She smiled saccharine sweet. 'We could see if our clothes are ready?'

He didn't seem to hear as he slid the rest of the apple into his mouth. Resting his forearms on raised knees, he slowly chewed, seemingly lost in his thoughts, even as his eyes searched hers. Then his head dropped back and he chuckled.

'Hey, remember the time when we—?'

She cut in. 'That's not a good idea.'

His brows knitted. 'What's not a good idea?'

'Reminiscing.'

'I was only going to say—' But he stopped. His big delectable chest expanded as he filled his lungs. 'You're right. We shouldn't bring up the past.'

But now he had her wondering. Was he about to mention their trip through the Hunter Valley when they'd stayed at that gorgeous Tudor-style bed and breakfast? Or the time they'd gone to an Australian Rules football game? Hardly a big sport fan, she'd nevertheless been swept up in the electric atmosphere of the enormous, cheering crowd and had applauded as loudly as Devlin when his team had won.

Or was he about to bring up the time his four-wheel drive got stuck in the deep dry sand on an island off Queensland? As night had fallen and shadows crept in, Devlin had built a fire. When a creature had rustled in the nearby brush—something huge, slimy and fanged, no doubt—he'd held her tight, murmuring in that rich, comforting voice that nothing would harm her.

'What are you smiling at?'

Brought back, she blinked over. 'I was smiling?'

'Yeah. You were.'

Then he smiled too, an encouraging soft tilt of his mouth, and she let go the breath burning in her lungs.

She'd thought it best not to communicate. She'd warned him not to reminisce. But, honestly, what harm could come from talking? He was well aware of the boundaries she'd put up. He'd put up his own. Both had agreed that it was best not to cross those lines again, no matter how tempting the prospect might be.

'I was thinking about the night we spent on that island,' she admitted, 'when I was scared of dingoes and lizards—'

'And we didn't get a wink of sleep.'

'But the fire was so warm and stars so bright…'

'When we got up you said you wanted to spend another night. I talked you into a swim at dawn.'

Her heartbeat began to gallop.

Not only had he talked her into an ocean dip, he'd talked her into doing it *naked*.

But Devlin didn't play on that part of the story. Rather he concentrated on the far wall, as if a screen were showing that scene from their past.

'The water was cool,' he recalled in a deep, far-off voice, 'so after our swim, we sprawled out on the sand.'

He stretched his bronzed arms high as though he'd been transported back and were soaking up the rays on that warm white sand now.

Caught up in the memory too, she added, 'We lay there, exhausted after our sleepless night, until the waves on high tide crept up and washed over our feet.'

'We stayed over that night, and the next night too.'

She smiled. 'And I wasn't scared at all.'

A knot of emotion caught in her chest. Taken aback, she bit her lip and averted her gaze.

She'd never questioned herself about Devlin before. But now for the first time she had to ask…had she acted rashly in ending their affair? Had she foreseen the outcome correctly? How could something so solid ultimately crack over time rather than get stronger? With all her heart she had believed she'd found The One. The man she would be with for ever.

But she hadn't mistaken the coolness that had settled in his eyes, in his touch, those last couple of weeks. In the end, after Scotland, it had almost been easier to admit the truth.

Devlin wasn't programmed for long term. He made his own rules. Lived life his way. Challenging. Daring.

He wasn't meant to be tied down.

When something warm and soft brushed her temple— a thrilling feather-light kiss—she bit her lip again, melting inside even while fighting to deny the desperate longing dripping through her veins.

Devlin's sultry voice murmured at her ear. 'I know what you're going to say. But seeing you again, being with you here now…'

She groaned and her heart squeezed more.

Why do this? Why couldn't he just let her be?

Shaking her head, she trembled and kept her gaze on the relative safety of the floor. 'No, Devlin, I don't—'

'Miss me? I think you do. And I missed you, Eden. The way you walk, the way you laugh.' The tip of his nose slid along the edge of her jaw. 'The way you smell.'

Her left side ignited like dry kindle touched by a lit match. Luckily she found the strength to turn and shove him away.

Or that was what she'd *meant* to do. But rather than repel him, her fingers dug into his hard, hot flesh as if mega-charged magnets were glued to their tips.

So close, his eyes burned like twilight-blue coals while his clean masculine scent burrowed under her skin.

'I said I wouldn't kiss you again, but I want to…' his head angled '…and way more than once.'

The delicious fire leapt high, consuming her inside and out. All the air—in the room, in her lungs—had evaporated. And her head…

Eden clamped her eyes shut.

Her head was *spinning*.

When his lips pressed against her fevered brow, her

pulse rate spiked three storeys. The rough of his chin drew a gentle circle over the spot, then trailed down the sweep of her nose, closer to her parted lips.

While her core throbbed a hot urgent beat, her fingers kneaded his chest more, pulling and pushing at the crisp hair and rock-solid flesh while his apple breath near her mouth hinted at the banquet of forbidden delights yet to come.

If she gave in.

His smile travelled over the hypersensitive slide of her lower lip. 'You're trembling, Eden, and not with anger.'

This was agony. Ecstasy.

Lunacy!

Exhibiting wills of their own, her fingers wove over his powerful bare chest, up the strong thick column of his neck. Curiously heavy yet also light, her head lolled sideways. 'This…can't happen.'

His nose nuzzled the shell of her ear. 'Remind me again why not.'

Her reasoning was slipping away, like lava melting down a hillside. 'Sleeping together is the easy part.'

His voice was thick. 'So very easy.'

'But we don't belong together.'

'Because I'm an insensitive, danger-hungry SOB and you're…' he nipped her lobe '…*paradise.*'

Her insides tugged and burned. 'I'm not exciting enough for you.'

'You're plenty exciting. I've never stopped wanting you. Is that a sin?'

'Yes,' she croaked as sizzling stars spun through her blood.

'When I saw you again today, I wanted to kidnap you. Or make love to you right there and then. Is that wrong?'

She hummed and sighed.

'Yes…'

He carefully turned her face to his. She dragged her eyes open and recognised his knowing, seductive smile.

'Eden, you keep saying yes.'

Did she?

She wanted to say *no*. She *must* say no. But as the word formed in her mind, his expert lips tasted her chin…her cheek…her slightly parted mouth. And she couldn't deny it any more because he must have felt her heart thumping the truth as she melted fully into his embrace.

Yes, yes…it told him.

Oh, God, yes.

CHAPTER FOUR

EDEN gazed into Devlin's hypnotic blue eyes and for the second time that day relented…to undeniable power…to the promise of his kiss. As he cupped her jaw her eyelids grew unspeakably heavy. His chest inflated, then he lightly touched his lips to hers.

Rather than the near-ravenous hunger with which he'd kissed her in the rain, this caress was a gentle graze, a preview of what his mouth could do given half the chance.

At the curling edges of her mind she knew the heat of his hand had left her face. His warm long fingers were splaying around her neck, winding up through her drying hair, holding her head steady as his purpose inch by inch grew stronger…minute by minute burned brighter.

On a sigh of welcome, her lips parted more and the full wonder of this joining gripped her, lifting her off the ground as if she were no more than a boneless puppet dangling from a string.

A rumbling growl worked up his throat as he set his weight carefully against hers until, tipping all the way back, she lay on the soft floor. He broke the kiss long enough to search her eyes, then he coiled his arm posses-

sively above her head and kissed her again, this time holding nothing back.

More than want, more than need…as his tongue wound
out to meet hers, their embrace linked them in ways more
than physical. Revisiting this rapture tasted sweeter than
she'd remembered, felt more exhilarating than she'd ever
dreamed. Like the old days, they existed in their own wonderful world, focused on enjoying the moment, then enjoying the next.

He dragged his knee up between her shins. As crisp hair
and steely heat tickled and rubbed her inside thigh, her
heart leapt and the juncture between her legs grew achingly
wet and warm. When her legs naturally parted, her arms
snaked around his neck and she arched against him,
needing to be closer than close.

Over the years, a quiet forbidden corner of her mind had
longed for this moment. The euphoric pleasure of Devlin's
body pressed like a human iron against hers…the whirling,
mind-blowing beat in the pit of her stomach as she antici-
pated the moment when he would fully take her…rock
her…*love* her…

As his knee pushed higher and his free hand travelled
down her side, across her quivering belly, between the
gaping folds of her robe, she imagined his length filling her,
stoking her again and again. She'd thought being with
Devlin now would be heaven, but heaven couldn't compare.

Maybe it was hell she was visiting. Enjoying such
reckless passion somehow didn't seem right. But anyone
who'd experienced this same kind of splendour wouldn't
condemn her. Who could blame her for hanging on now,
submitting to the fire, while they waited for…?

Her mind stuttered, wound back.

They were waiting for…?

Her stomach muscles clutched and eyes flew open as the tail end of the thought lashed her like a whip. Snapping her head to one side, she severed the kiss and gasped for air.

'Devlin, we can't do this!'

He caught her face and urged her gaze to meet his. Open amusement gleamed in his curious eyes. 'Eden, love, we're beyond that.'

He nipped her lower lip. The tip of his tongue tasted the kiss-swollen flesh before his mouth closed over hers again. As his body moved up and over hers, scorching desire blew into an uncontrollable inferno set to consume her.

But…

With a huge lump in her throat, she caught his shoulders and managed to push him back an inch. 'We can't make love here in Sabrina and Nathan's suite, especially not on the *floor*.'

His amused look buckled. 'They're not due back for ages.' He tickled her nose with his. 'They don't need to know.'

Wiggling out from beneath him, she sat up, brought her knees together and made a tight cocoon of her robe. 'What if they arrive early and find us here, like *this*?'

Eden's parents had their children late in life. While loving, they supported the view that kids should be seen and not heard. Until they'd left home, the girls had shared a room and, in many ways, the elder sister had become the younger one's role model. Sabrina reminded Eden so much of her younger self…eager and starry-eyed. Consequently, in recent years, she'd warned her sister never to let passion rule her head.

Eden had issued some less than complimentary remarks about Devlin in the past. If Sabrina walked in now and witnessed this scene, she'd lose all respect for her.

Devlin's gaze skated from Eden's to the door. He cringed as if imagining it bursting open and their siblings striding in. His mouth swung to one side and he nodded.

'You're right. Wouldn't look good.' He sprang to his feet with the agility of a jungle cat and swept her up too.

'Where are we going?'

His grin spread wide. 'Where do you think?'

'The bedroom?'

Standing front to front, he double cupped her bottom and pressed her pelvis against his. 'Yes, ma'am.'

She melted at the feel of his erection beneath his towel, burning against her robed belly. She lost her breath imagining the delicious wonders he could perform between the sheets, coaxing her body to heights that left her unspeakably dizzy.

And yet…

Her chest squeezing, she looked at him with pleading eyes. 'We can't use the bedroom.'

The grip on her rump tightened and his shadowed jaw shifted. 'What do you mean we can't use the bedroom? That's what bedrooms are for.'

He was thinking like a man. She wanted to think like a man too. But, 'It's *their* bedroom, not ours.'

'Ah, but you're forgetting, there are *two* rooms. They can't use both—not at the same time, anyway.'

She thought it through and hazarded a smile. 'I guess.'

He took her hand and ushered her towards the opened bedroom door. 'The room I changed in looked like the main suite. We'll go in here.' He cocked his chin at the room she'd used earlier.

Before she could reply, he gathered her near again. Capturing her mouth with his, he reversed them both towards the bedroom. Falling under his spell once more, she clutched onto his shoulders, unable to stem the moan of pure want building in her chest, pushing up her throat. As if remembering something ultra important, he broke the kiss and, holding her eyes determinedly, rested his forehead against hers.

'Have I mentioned that I've missed you?'

His voice was so gravelled and honest, moisture sprang to her eyes. She surrendered a faint smile and admitted the truth.

'I've missed you too.'

His pupils dilated before a possessive sound vibrated beneath her fingers and he claimed her mouth again.

Now he moved faster, blindly towing her along, kissing her in heated snatches as they knocked into the side table, collided with some potted plant. When they smacked into the door frame, their kiss dissolved on laughter.

With a pained grin, he rubbed a spot on his thigh. 'At this rate, we'll leave here covered in bruises and demolish the place to boot.'

Taking charge, he swept her up into his arms and strode into the centre of the bedroom where he set her down as if she were as fragile as a glass figurine. With his gaze lingering over the curve of her neck, with the tension and sexual need spiralling higher and tighter, he eased the robe off her shoulders.

She let her eyes drift closed, her head arced back and she melted into the moment. Her skin, her breasts—exposed to the air and his eyes—felt on fire while a kernel of want glowed hot and deliciously deep inside. Undiluted bliss awaited her, the kind of Nirvana she hadn't thought she'd know again… Devlin ready and eager to add fuel to these rekindled flames. But still…

She expelled a breath and grudgingly opened her eyes. It was no use. No matter how she tried, no matter how much she wanted to, she simply *couldn't* push aside the niggling image of her baby sister walking through that door.

She murmured against Devlin's lips as his chest grazed her painfully tight nipples and he prepared to devour her again. 'I'm sorry. I don't feel right here either.'

'I beg to differ.' His hands sculpted the length of her arms, to where the robe had caught at her elbows. 'You feel sensational.'

Ditto a thousand times over, but, 'I can't relax. What if they knock on the door?'

'It's their place,' he said absently, tasting the corner of her mouth. 'They'll have their own key.'

'I mean what if they knock on the *bedroom* door?'

Chuckling in the rich, wicked way that made her tummy flutter and swoop, he kissed her neck. 'Why the devil would they do that?'

'It's not so out of the question. What if we've picked the wrong bedroom and they don't know we're here and just walk in?'

His head slowly pulled back. 'We'll lock the door.'

His expression had lost its humour. But she wasn't making excuses. If this had been *their* suite, if they hadn't been waiting for the siblings to show up with important news, if she'd never contacted Devlin in the first place with that scheme to save Sabrina's heart—

Wincing, Eden lowered her gaze from his.

What on earth had she started? Letting this go any further wasn't a good idea. In fact, it was a darn *bad* one. Not only was she opening herself up to more heartache, she was risking the loss of her sister's respect.

Heart sinking, she pulled the robe back up her arms and edged away. 'Maybe we should forget it.'

He spun her back. '*Can* you forget it, Eden?'

She held his intense gaze and trembled. Succumbing to forces far stronger than her insecurities, she sighed.

'No.'

'Neither can I.' A muscle in his jaw ticced before he surrendered to a patient smile. 'I have an idea.'

She darted a look over his shoulder and made her objection clear. 'The balcony's out.'

His eyes widened with interest. 'That's a pity, but my thought was the bathroom.'

Without giving her time to consider, he took her hand and ushered her into the adjoining room.

Filled with water, the sunken bath would pass for a mini lake. Bevel-edged mirrors lined almost every wall. The soft blooms of crimson roses and stalks of lavender, arranged in tall crystal vases, contrasted with the gleaming surfaces of black Italian marble and squeaky clean glass.

He spun the lock, then held her again, his adamant hands on her hips this time. He arched a brow and grinned. 'Now where were we?'

As their lips met again he fisted the towelling near her neck and dragged her robe unremittingly down until it pooled on the floor.

Releasing the anxious tension, she groaned on a smile. *If you can't beat 'em...*

Tugging at his towel, she found her tiptoes and murmured against his scratchy chin, only half serious this time. 'They might hear us.'

Throwing open the shower door, he flicked the tap and

water hissed from twin nozzles full bore. A cloud of perfumed steam plumed around them.

'There.' He grinned slowly. 'No one will hear a thing.'

'They'll think we're having a shower together.'

With deliberate purpose, his mouth sampled the sweep of her shoulder. 'Give me enough time, they'll be right.'

'I don't think—'

He growled against her lips, *'No more thinking.'* Then in a rough but beguiling voice, he murmured, 'No more talking.'

With steam misting the mirror, heating his skin, Devlin set his hands around Eden's slender waist and hoisted her up onto the marble vanity. Shivering, she sat up ramrod straight, her tawny-tipped nipples standing up too as goose bumps erupted over her silky skin.

'Hey,' she cried. 'That's cold.'

Fatally drawn, he lowered his head and caressed her breasts with his mouth, looping his tongue around each hardened peak, grazing his teeth over the sensitive beaded tips.

The emotion was easy to describe. He'd died and gone to heaven. She must've felt somewhat the same because in no time at all she loosened up against him.

As her fingers slipped through his hair he grinned and flicked his tongue again. 'I gather you're warming up.'

She drew one knee high until her inside thigh rubbed his shoulder. 'Mmm, nicely, thank you.'

Her purred admission tripped another wire and his testosterone gauge leapt to a new and volatile place. He found her hand and moulded her palm around his near-explosive length. What was it about Eden that was so special? So…necessary?

'See what you do to me?' he growled.

In response, she squeezed a long blissful groan from him.

'Over this steam, I can't see too much at all.' She funnelled her tight-fisted grip first up then down his pulsing shaft. 'But I certainly can *feel*.' She craned up and snatched a kiss from his lips. 'Let's make use of that fluffy rug on the floor over there?'

'This position suits me fine for the moment.'

She laughed. 'As long as I don't get pins and needles.'

'Let me take your mind off your seat.'

His breathing deeper now, his heart rate ratcheting up another rung, he trailed moist, teasing kisses between her breasts, down to her belly, the way she'd always done for him. When her thigh near his head relaxed and dropped slightly open, he wound that leg over his shoulder. Balance seemed a good idea, so he wound her other leg over too.

Hunkering down, he curled his arms around her legs then, savouring every second, he fanned his fingers over her belly. The pads of each thumb traced down through her soft curls until they parted the silken valley of her folds. His heart thumping against his ribs, he used the tip of his nose to circle her exposed bud.

Gasping, she fisted her hands in his hair.

She got her breath back enough to sigh, 'I wouldn't do that again if I were you.'

This time he circled the sensitive spot with the stiffened tip of his tongue.

While he groaned with satisfaction, she shuddered against him at the same time her legs coiled possessively in, her heels riding his back.

'I need you inside me, Devlin,' she demanded. 'I need you there now.'

Amidst the clouds of steam, he continued to massage and tease her with his hands, with his tongue.

When next she spoke, her voice sounded drugged and desperate. 'You're not listening to me.'

'I'm hearing every word. You want me inside you.'

She moaned, glad he finally understood. 'Yes, yes. Lift me down.'

His tongue trailed a deep line up her glistening centre. The fresh feminine taste of her hit him low in the gut and, although he'd promised himself he would prolong every step, now his mischievous side wanted to bring her hazardously close to the edge.

Tenderly, earnestly, he kissed her long…kissed her deep.

She was clutching the vanity at her sides when he reluctantly came away. Rewarded by this picture of her genuine abandon, his blood heated more and he smiled.

'Is that better?'

'No.' She pushed his head down again. 'You missed a spot.'

He wanted to laugh. Far be it from him to complain.

Too soon, her muscles contracted and her thighs viced. When she spasmed and cried out, he placed his mouth fully over her again and, holding nothing back, propelled her that much higher, wanting her that much more.

Next time he would love her longer, draw her delight out more, but for now…

Her grip on his head loosened as she grew deliciously limp. He carefully lowered her legs from around his shoulders and focused on the satiated sight of her, slouched against the wall-to-wall mirror. Naked. Vulnerable.

Beyond tempting.

He moved to take her, make love to her the old-fashioned

way. But, remembering in time, he shook himself and instead brushed aside strands of golden hair hanging over her eyes.

'I need to leave you for a minute.'

Her expression was dreamy. 'Leave. Why?'

'Protection.' He kept condoms in his wallet. 'I'll be back in ten seconds.' He ran his lips over the shell of her ear. When her arms snaked around his neck to hold him close, he contained the dangerous surge of desire and stepped away. 'Make that five seconds.'

His towel on the floor, he hightailed it out of the bathroom, out the bedroom door, and spied his wallet on the table. At the same moment he dived on the leather, found the wrap, he caught a movement out the corner of his eye.

Heart lurching, he wheeled around.

His brother stood by the door. Nate's wide-eyed girlfriend stood beside him.

CHAPTER FIVE

NATE scratched his jaw, no doubt trying to hide the single deep dimple that belied his serious tone.

'Devlin, this is...' his mouth twitched '...a surprise.'

Devlin stood stock-still as Sabrina's startled gaze travelled up from his thighs to his frozen expression. Her delicate face pale against her long brown hair, she held onto Nate and wobbled out an uncertain smile.

'You must be Devlin. P-pleased to meet you.'

Manners returning, she took a step forward, hand outstretched. When she faltered, dropped her hand and stepped awkwardly back, Devlin slid a dining chair strategically before him.

Should he make a joke? Because this was funny, right? Eden would have a great big laugh over this. They'd both laugh about it.

One day.

'And you're Sabrina.' Devlin manufactured a light smile that almost worked with the casual shoulder shrug. 'Might be best if we shake hands later.'

'I'm guessing Eden is through there—' Nate raised a brow '—having a shower?'

Devlin explained. 'We got caught in the rain, were both

soaked through, so we gave Housekeeping our things and that's why I'm not wearing any…' he lowered his voice '…any, uh, clothes.'

Laughter shone in Nate's eyes. But he cleared his throat and gave a solemn nod. 'I see.'

'Sorry we kept you waiting,' Sabrina chipped in, still clinging to Nate.

Devlin waved the apology away. 'We kept ourselves busy.'

Sabrina merely blinked. She was in shock. It wasn't every day you walked in on your sister's ex standing bare-butt naked in the living room.

Linking his arm through Sabrina's, Nate ushered her towards the view. 'Why don't you tell Eden we're here, Dev?' Nate's eyes twinkled with a message. *Don't rush. Take your time.*

As they passed Devlin gripped the back of chair. He'd burned a candle for Eden in the months following their break-up. Nate was only being supportive and understanding now. Clearly his brother saw this situation as a victory. In a way it was. He hadn't felt this invigorated—this *connected*—in a very long while.

Still, something in his brother's attitude rubbed Devlin the wrong way. He knew how this looked—alone together for an hour and he'd coaxed Eden out of her clothes. But he hadn't twisted her arm, only convinced her that they wouldn't be caught.

He shoved the chair out the way.

How would he ever break this to her?

While Nate kept Sabrina occupied, showing her the ferry traffic churning white-water trails across the harbour, Devlin strode back towards the bathroom. He had to let

Eden know that her nightmare-of-sorts had come true. They'd been sprung.

Bad.

But when he re-entered the steam-filled room, any thought of siblings and conscience disappeared. On the white centre rug, Eden lay splayed out on her back, one knee raised, her arms draped over her head. Visible through the mist, her fingers wiggled at him.

'Let me have it,' she cooed.

Hooked and desperately wanting to be landed, he moved closer as she edged up onto an elbow. Her long blonde hair slid over her shoulder, her breast.

'The condom,' she explained, her fingertips trailing his shin. 'I'll slip it on.'

The condom wrap crinkled in his closed palm.

In the whole scheme of things, what would another five minutes matter? Everyone knew what was going on here. What any thinking person *knew* would happen if he and Eden were alone for any reasonable length of time.

S.E.X.

If he told Eden that Sabrina was outside, would they ever finish this? Because, make no mistakes, 'this' *deserved* to be finished.

But as he hunkered down Eden sat up, sudden worry flashing in her eyes. Guess she'd read his expression, his hesitation.

Her voice was threadbare. 'What's wrong?'

His gut kicked. Of course he had to tell her. As much as he'd like to ignore it for five minutes more, that wasn't an option. Still, he wasn't looking forward to her reaction.

When she continued to search his eyes, he wove a

knuckle around her satiny cheek and confessed, 'Our guests have arrived.'

Her expression stilled. Then she swore. Then she scrambled like a madwoman to grab her nearby robe and hold it to her breasts. As she took in his naked body her colourless lips gaped open.

'Please tell me Sabrina didn't see you like that?'

Okay. 'Sabrina didn't see me like this.'

She bit off a cry of panic and dropped her head into her hands. 'I should never have taken the chance. Murphy's law said they'd arrive early. How will I ever face Sabrina?' she mumbled through a spread of fingers.

His brow knitted.

He sympathised, but, really, was it *that* bad? You'd think she'd just lost her virginity to the devil himself and all the angels in heaven were about to pass judgement. All they'd done was have a little fun. If anything was depressing, it was that their fun had been interrupted.

'Sabrina's an adult,' he reminded her, 'like you and I were adults when we were twenty-one. She'll understand.' He pushed to his feet, summed up the area, their state of undress. 'Admittedly, this isn't the ideal way to meet, but think about it… After this, how much easier will it be for them to tell us their news?'

Whatever the hell it was.

She found his gaze, her eyes bright with shame.

'But what will I tell her?' she whispered.

'She won't expect excuses.'

She was a woman in love. Happy couples only wanted to spread their sunshine around. Whenever one of his friends tied the knot, the outcome was always the same…

his bachelor buddies became married matchmakers. Much to Devlin's consternation, he was usually a target.

A series of emotions faded in and out of Eden's face. Comprehension, acceptance, hope. Devlin offered a smile and his hand. Dragging her to her feet was like pulling an anchor.

While she took her time sliding back into her robe, he knocked off the water. The hiss died but the room was a sauna. All that lovely steam gone to waste.

'There's another courtesy robe on the rack,' she muttered, 'if you'd like to wear more than a towel.'

He recognised his misty reflection in the mirror—well over a head taller than Eden, naked as the day he'd greeted the world. Lucky poor Sabrina hadn't fainted.

He swung the robe down and, having covered himself, held Eden's gaze as well as her shoulders. 'You ready?'

'No.' Her mouth quivered before she smiled. 'Let's face the music anyway.'

Filling her lungs, Eden squared her shoulders and, stomach churning like a cement mixer, walked out into the main room, Devlin at her side. Sabrina stood by the window with Nathan, late afternoon sunlight illuminating their frames.

Unaware of their company, Sabrina gazed at Nathan as he pointed toward the Vaucluse cliffs, her face so innocent and brimming with happiness. It was like going back in time. Once she'd looked at Devlin that way. Besotted. Blind. And Devlin was still Devlin. Dangerous, irresistible, and better than ever. Didn't mean he was good for her.

In fact, quite the opposite.

She'd done a foolish thing, falling for his charm and acting on physical attraction when she'd told him point blank to stay away. He'd hurt her before. They had no future now.

And yet…

She couldn't punish herself over their encounter in the bathroom. Her life was a well-structured, carefully organised calendar of events. She left nothing to chance. When was the last time she'd done something off the wall? *Years.* Didn't mean she wanted to continue being reckless.

She most certainly didn't want Sabrina to be.

Sabrina caught sight of her and broke into a my-world-is-complete smile. She ran forward, arms outstretched.

'Eden.' She hugged her sister fiercely and murmured against her ear, 'Thanks for coming. This worked out better than we'd planned.'

Doubt and curiosity flooded Eden's mind.

Good news was Sabrina didn't hate her. Bad news?

Surely this rendezvous hadn't been a set-up to get her and Devlin back together. And Sabrina was reading way too much into what had occurred behind closed bathroom doors. Sabrina had always hinted that she should've given Devlin another chance. But this was hardly a new start. It was more…an encore.

Before Eden could respond, Sabrina pulled back, her face lit with joy and pride.

'This is Nathan. He's been dying to meet you. Nate—' she waved her boyfriend over '—this is Eden.'

Joining them, he took her hand. 'Great to meet you.'

His hand was big and warm like Devlin's. He looked like Devlin too—tall, dark with a similar muscular frame and a lopsided smile that said, 'You can trust me'. Of course Sabrina would find him irresistible…as had all the girls who had come before her.

'Sorry we held you up,' Nathan said to them both. 'My house alarm went off. There's been a few bad burglaries in the area. I wanted to make sure everything was secure.'

Eden exhaled. She'd have done the same thing, and of course Sabrina would've accompanied her boyfriend rather than stay here to face them alone. Whatever it was they wanted to share, they wanted to share it together.

'Perhaps we ought to sit down?' Devlin said in a let's-pretend-everything's-hunky-dory tone.

'A drink, anyone?' Nathan pitched in, moving towards the bar.

'*No.*' Inwardly cringing, Eden pressed her lips together. She'd spoken way too loud, too urgently, but the simple truth was, 'I'm eager to hear your news.'

She tried to sound enthusiastic, encouraging. But beneath the upbeat façade, she was ready to hyperventilate. Was she soon to be an auntie? Was a wedding gift in order? Although, looking now, Sabrina's finger didn't boast any telltale rings.

Sabrina's gaze searched out Nathan's, who crossed back from the bar to rejoin her. She nibbled her lip, her pale blue eyes glittering with uncertainty and something akin to fear.

Eden's insides looped with a sickening knot and she found Sabrina's hand. 'It's okay, honey. Whatever it is…' *if you're having a baby* '…I'm here for you.'

Devlin held his brother's shoulder. 'Same goes for me.'

Sabrina squeezed Eden's hand then dragged in a big breath. 'Well, here goes.' She rushed it out. 'I'm moving in with Nate.'

Time seemed to stretch out before folding in over itself like layers of thick messy syrup. Tugging her ear, feeling strangely light-headed, Eden coughed out a guarded laugh.

'I'm not sure I heard right.'

'That's *it*?' Devlin sounded relieved.

Nathan coiled his arm around Sabrina's waist and urged her close. 'We want to start moving her personal things out tomorrow.'

The protective lioness inside Eden leapt up and snarled. *Do you, now?*

She crossed her arms. 'What about your studies, Sabrina?'

'But I'm almost done,' Sabrina exclaimed. 'Just this year to go and I'll never have to look at another university assignment question again.'

Eden elaborated. 'This year, your *final* year, is as important as any other. If you fail a subject, you'll have to re-enrol. That could mean another six months.'

Since primary school Sabrina had wanted to be a teacher, but university students on the home stretch sometimes ran out of puff. Sabrina had neglected her studies since meeting Nathan. If she failed a subject or two, she might not return to finish her degree. In six months Nathan wouldn't give a dry fig if Sabrina dropped out for love of him. He'd have moved on to his next conquest.

Sabrina's mouth bowed, but then her chin kicked up.

'I won't fail.' She wrapped her arms around Nate's hips, nuzzling under his arm against his chest. 'That's why I'm moving in. We'll be together all the time.'

Defeat prickled behind Eden's eyes. Why were women so trusting? So gullible?

She spoke quietly, calmly, even while pieces of her seemed to break away. 'How is being together all the time the answer?'

Sabrina tsked, as if her next reply would make it all so clear. 'I won't need to take time out from study for us to see each other. Nate even said he'd help with assignments.'

Wonderful. Nathan obviously knew heaps about ancient history and the English canon.

Nathan spoke up. 'We wanted to tell you together because...' His sombre gaze mellowed. 'Well, because of your past. We knew this would be awkward for you both, but we wanted everything out in the open, and we wanted to do it with all four of us in a secure but neutral setting.'

Hands low on his hips, Devlin nodded as if Nathan were on his way to solving all the problems of the world. 'We appreciate it—don't we, Eden?'

Eden's throat burned.

She would agree. She *must* agree.

But the accusation tumbled out. 'Sabrina, you're making a mistake.'

As Sabrina's face crumpled Devlin said out of the side of his mouth, 'It's their business, remember?'

A suffocating lump clogged her throat. Yeah, it was their business until the love shack fell apart, then it was big-sister-mopping-up-the-mess business.

'I'll take good care of Sabrina.' Nathan looked longingly into Sabrina's eyes, then dropped a kiss on her brow. 'I care very deeply for your sister.'

'Not enough to put a ring on her finger.'

Eden heard the venom in her own voice and her face flamed. But it was too late to take it back, and the sick ache in her stomach said that her sister was being...exploited might be too strong a word. Manipulated suited better. Nathan was eager to have Sabrina in a relationship, in his environment, in his bed every night. If Sabrina were older, wiser, Eden would've accepted the news, even after six short weeks of dating.

But Sabrina was young, naïve, as hopelessly in love as

Eden had once been with Devlin. She knew precisely the absolute and urgent nature of Sabrina's feelings, as if she would die if she couldn't be with the one she loved. But Eden felt it in her gut, with every instinct she possessed…Nathan would tire of Sabrina and her baby sister would be left heartbroken, and who knew for how long?

As Nathan straightened to his full height Sabrina's wounded look hardened into wilfulness. 'I don't *want* to get married. I just want to be with my boyfriend every chance we get. You remember what that's like, don't you, Eden?'

Her plaintive gaze flicked to Devlin.

Eden arched a brow. Yes, she remembered too well. That was the problem.

The doorbell rang. Needing to cool down, Eden mumbled, 'I'll get it,' and moved off. Thankfully it was Housekeeping delivering their freshly pressed clothes.

When Eden rejoined the trio, two sets of clothing draped over her arm, she'd regained her composure. Histrionics were never useful. Devlin had his faults but in this he was right. She'd done all she could but at the end of the day it was Sabrina's life. Sadly, she'd have to make her own mistakes and learn from them like anyone else. Eden couldn't save Sabrina from every hurt, no matter how much she wanted to.

She kissed Sabrina's cheek and with a supportive smile said, 'We'll get dressed and leave you and Nathan to enjoy your night together.'

Sabrina's eyes sparkled with hope. 'So you're okay with me moving out of our apartment?'

Eden thought of the scene in the bathroom, of how Sabrina must know at least some of what had transpired.

Irrespective of age, if Sabrina was being foolish, this afternoon her older sister had been more so. She couldn't be a hypocrite.

Eden shrugged good-humouredly. 'If you're happy, honey, I'm happy.'

Sabrina's brows pushed in and up. 'Oh, I am, Eden. I'm so happy, I could burst.'

Eden held her smile, then pivoted away before Sabrina saw the moisture welling in her eyes. Devlin followed her into the bedroom and clicked the door closed.

Numb inside, she stepped into her laundered panties. 'This is worse than I thought.'

Devlin grunted. 'Not from where I'm standing.'

Eden bristled. Of course he'd think that way. Little brother had got himself a beautiful young woman to share his bed every night—for however long it lasted.

'He'll break her heart.' Feeling sickeningly resigned to the fact, she dragged out her bra.

His voice held an edge. 'Eden, they're in love.'

Yeah, well, they'd been in love once too. Correction. *She'd* been in love. Devlin had been in lust. After that erotic bathroom scene, had anything changed?

He sat down on the bed and urged her to sit too. Wanting to cry, she sank down heavily.

'I'll sound like Freud's sidekick,' he said, 'but it's obvious what's going on. You're letting our past relationship—your misgivings about me—colour your opinion here.'

Eden held her hollow stomach as a tear slid down her cheek. Her heart had been ripped out when they'd broken up. She didn't want Sabrina enduring that same horrible pain. And yet given Nathan's reputation with women, Sabrina had exactly that to look forward to.

Devlin settled his hand on her lap. The heat did little to warm her. 'We'll go somewhere quiet and talk—'

'I don't want to talk,' she ground out. *I don't want to look back.* 'Look what happens when we start to talk.'

'We get along.'

She pushed to her feet. 'If that's what you want to call it.'

'So that's it?'

Showing him her back, she dragged her dress out of its cover. 'I told you, I don't want to discuss it.'

'People who date sometimes stay together and sometimes they move on.'

She sent him an arch look. 'Gee, thank you, Dr Phil.'

'That's why couples move in together, to see if they fit. Nate and Sabrina are mature enough to know the score. You'd do better to accept your sister's situation rather than tear yourself up over it.'

Feeling empty inside, Eden clutched the dress to her chest. She hated that he made so much sense. She only wanted Sabrina to be happy. Damn it, *she* wanted to be happy too.

She rotated back and questioned his eyes, which were all the more sexy because he was brooding.

Was his suggestion to go somewhere and talk just a line? An excuse to get her alone and finish what they'd started?

Her frustration and hurt over how they'd parted had been bottled up for so long. She couldn't deny that being with Devlin again—enjoying his unique brand of masculine sensuality and affection—had smoothed away some of that torment. As shocking as it was to accept, the bare-faced truth was…

Sighing, she dropped the dress onto the bed.

Maybe talking with him more—finishing what they'd started—*wouldn't* be a mistake. Maybe it was precisely what she needed to exorcise her demons. Maybe she deserved one glorious night of get-it-out-of-your-system sex and to hell with tomorrow.

Eden wasn't desperate for marriage. Plenty of women chose not to marry these days, or not until they were older. Three years ago she'd worn rose-coloured glasses, but now her eyes were wide open. She and Devlin were attracted to each other, enjoyed each other's company. Maybe it wasn't for ever, but it certainly was formidable.

She should take a leaf from her younger sister's book for a change and simply live life. Hold onto the spark today had ignited. Enjoy the moment.

Take a risk.

Filling her lungs, Eden nodded. 'We'll go somewhere…and talk.'

His grave expression eased. He stood and brought her close, holding her the way he had that night on the beach—tenderly, protectively.

As if he wouldn't let anything harm her.

His warm breath brushed her hair as his clean musky scent coated her senses. 'You're doing the right thing.'

Resignation dropped through her.

He didn't understand. This wasn't about right or wrong. She didn't have a choice. It was either see this through to its natural conclusion or regret she hadn't for the rest of her life.

But, if she was pushing forward with extending this rendezvous—if she intended to take this all the way—she'd make damn sure she enjoyed it.

CHAPTER SIX

TEN minutes later, he and Eden had said goodbye to Sabrina and Nate, and were exiting one of the hotel's ground-floor lifts. Crossing the wide expanse of shiny marble floor, with a baby grand tinkling on the mezzanine floor above, Eden stopped and wove her fingers up his lapels.

'So tell me…where do you plan to take me?'

As her expectant eyes sparkled up at him Devlin thanked his lucky stars. Given the intensity of their attraction for each other, it was no surprise how they'd ended up together in that bathroom. But after the way Eden had taken Sabrina and Nate's news—hardly well—he'd doubted she'd be in any kind of mood to continue with the more intimate side of this reunion.

Yet ultimately she hadn't decided to close up, shut him out and walk away. She'd accepted, on some level at least, their siblings' decision and had gone one step further.

She'd agreed to his suggestion that they talk.

Smiling at her now, he covered her hands with his. 'Where would you like to go?'

Her gaze slid towards the dark granite reservations desk. 'Why don't you get a room?'

Amidst streams of guests, strolling to the bank of lifts,

sauntering towards the à la carte restaurant, Devlin felt his testosterone levels surge. He liked this new Eden, or rather he liked having the old Eden back. Other than her cheeks looking a little flushed, she appeared cool, in complete control. She was making no bones about it. She was ready to dive straight back under the proverbial covers.

However, 'When I said we'd go somewhere quiet,' he said lightly, 'I didn't necessarily mean another hotel suite.'

She shrugged. 'I did.'

His chin tucked in but then he laughed. She wasn't messing around.

His hands left hers to shape over her slender shoulders. 'Are you sure that's what you want?'

She gave a decisive nod.

'You want a room here,' he qualified, slanting his head, 'knowing Nate and Sabrina are in the same building?'

It was her turn to laugh.

'Now look who's being neurotic.' Then her eyes clouded, the apple green turning grey. 'Isn't this what you want?'

Having her in his arms again? Hell, yes. But, 'That's not the point.'

'Then I'm not sure what the point is.'

He found and kissed her palm. 'Want a hint?'

One side of her mouth lifted. 'Sure.'

'A leisurely walk through The Rocks, or a ferry ride to Manly. But dinner first, somewhere casual and fun.'

Her frown returned. 'You're hungry again?'

He grinned. 'Eden, there's something else couples might do over dinner.'

She wet her lips as if she were suddenly nervous. 'Well, I've read about it…but I don't think I'd be into sex in public places—'

Interesting thought, but, 'Try again.'

She seemed to think it through before her shoulders sagged. 'You mean you *really* want to talk.'

Hadn't he said that in the first place? He arched a brow. 'Don't sound so thrilled.'

Her hands twined up around his neck. 'I want to do more than talk.'

'I do too.' A society couple walked past and he lowered his voice. 'But I want to be certain it's for the right reasons.'

'How many reasons are there?'

His jaw shifted as he took her hands from his lapels and held them firmly between them.

Being cautious earlier was one thing, but if anyone had said he would ever second-guess this kind of blatant invitation to make love with the lady whose memory had haunted him for three long years he'd have had them certified.

Kissing her this afternoon in the rain had been unavoidable. Their brief sojourn in the bathroom was superb. But a quickie in some hotel room with a hasty goodbye tagged on the end didn't work for him. Not with any woman, particularly not Eden.

His gaze wandered to an arrangement of soaring potted palms, their fronds rustling gently in the air-con breeze, and an idea struck, as powerful and illuminating as a lightning bolt.

With her hands in his, he encircled her waist and brought her close.

'Take some time off next week,' he said. 'Come away with me for a couple of days. I'll collect you at nine tomorrow. You can be back at work by Tuesday.'

Her stupefied gaze hunted his face. 'You really want to

wait?' Then, teasing, she narrowed her eyes. 'Are you sure
your name's Devlin Stone?'

Devin blinked. It wasn't a big sting, but it was a sting
nonetheless.

'I haven't changed.' Eden had always meant far more
to him than a sleeping partner. Didn't she know that?

Doubt dimmed the light in her eyes. 'Maybe you're
hoping I'll get cold feet?'

'I'm praying that you don't.'

He wasn't trying to shake her off. Actually, he wasn't
certain what would come of this. He only knew he wanted
to make the most of it, for both their sakes. What they'd
enjoyed today was special. Had to be or she wouldn't be so
eager to be with him again. As eager as he was to be with her.

But if he was going to do this, he'd do it right.

'Is there anyone you need to organise to get the time
off?' he asked, thinking, too, it would be better if she wasn't
home when Nate moved Sabrina's things out.

Eden's mouth dropped open. 'You're serious, aren't you?'

In what might've been a dance move, he swirled her
under his arm and ushered her towards the door.

'I'll see you home,' he said, accompanying her out into
the hotel's forecourt where silver-service taxis awaited.
'On the way I'll tell you what you need to bring.'

Eden was still dazed when the cab pulled up outside her
apartment building. After Sabrina's news—that she
planned to move out and live with Nathan—Eden had
analysed her own feelings for Devlin more deeply and was
surprised to discover she wanted to go the whole nine yards.

Having come this far, if she didn't sleep with Devlin
now she'd regret it. She needed closure. Enjoying him one

last time, as she'd dreamed of so often, was the answer. She was certain.

But that didn't necessarily mean she wanted to go overboard and escape with him for two whole days to some mystery destination. During the cab ride here, he'd suggested she pack a swimsuit, some light summer clothes and a hat. She guessed he had some beach up north in mind.

Would making a weekend of it overly complicate matters as she suspected it would? Bottom line, she wanted to get him out of her system and as soon as possible. After the deed was done—after they'd made love the way they used to and her pent-up frustration was spent—she'd be free to get on with her life as Devlin would no doubt get on with his, just like last time when she'd made clear they were over.

So was her answer to his getaway question yes or no?

He slid from the cab, then helped her out. She tried to straighten her poor dress, which had shrunk a size and now sat well above the knee.

'Would you like to come up for a coffee?' she ventured.

With a bedroom nearby, he might forget about 'doing it right' in favouring of 'doing it now'. Then she wouldn't have to worry about whether going away with him was risky or merely necessary.

The sun had only moments ago set. In the misty circle of a street lamp, his eyes flashed before he grinned, as if he'd guessed the motive behind her invitation for coffee. The message in his eyes was clear. If he was going to have her, he'd have her on his terms.

'Not tonight,' he said. 'You need to make some phone calls, pack some things.'

She held her stomach as it somersaulted.

This was crunch time. Would she really go through with

what promised to be a two-day, solely her and Devlin, romantic adventure? Today he'd seemed the same charming Devlin and yet he'd changed too. He looked more mature. Felt even more dangerous. Would daring a full forty-eight hours with Devlin mean resuming control of her life—her past—or playing with a fire that wouldn't want to be doused?

He brushed a kiss against her cheek that dipped and lingered near her mouth. His smooth rich voice caused the fine hairs on her arm to quiver.

'I'll be here at nine,' he said, making the decision for her before sliding back into the taxi. 'Don't forget the sunscreen.'

In her apartment a few minutes later, Eden heeled off her still-damp shoes and headed for her phone. No use delaying. She had to make that call about clearing Monday or she might chicken out. And now Devlin had set a time— now his proposition had come this far—dodging the bullet didn't seem to be an option.

If the price of redemption was two days of sexual bliss, well, guess she'd just have to grin and bear it.

Her assistant from Temptations picked up her home extension on the third ring. Eden imagined Tracey Hardon's chocolate-brown eyes widen beneath her dead-straight brunette fringe.

'Eden? It's Saturday night. What's up?'

'I won't be in on Monday.'

'Are you ill?'

'Having a long weekend.'

'Hmm, sounds interesting.'

Eden grunted. 'Hopefully.'

'Want to share?'

Clamping the receiver between ear and shoulder, Eden sucked in her tummy and slid down the dress's side zip. 'Just going away for a couple of days.'

'With a man?'

Eden stopped unzipping. 'How did you guess?'

'Because it's about time.'

Wandering to the living-room window to make doubly sure the taxi had departed—that Devlin hadn't changed his mind about her coffee-with-cream invite—she said a little indignantly, 'I've dated before.'

'And I can't remember the last time you had fun. This guy must be special.'

'He was,' Eden grudgingly admitted.

The connection fell quiet before a splutter came down the line. 'Don't tell me…this doesn't involve that hunk you dated years ago. Devlin someone?'

Tracey was a friend as well as employee. But Eden hadn't told her about Sabrina dating Nathan, or her idea to discuss and rectify that situation with Devlin today. She'd hoped the meeting would all go to plan and no one would need be the wiser.

Man, had she got that wrong.

Eden dropped the curtain and sank onto the couch. 'It's not what you think.'

'I'm thinking this sounds *fabulous*. They say you never get over your first love.'

Eden sniffed. Just who were *they* anyway?

She fell back against the cushions and wiggled her toes. 'It's only a couple of days. No big deal.'

'If you want my opinion—'

Eden's mouth crimped into a grin. 'As if you won't give it to me anyway.'

'I say go for it! Take the whole *week* off. You haven't had a vacation since I've known you.'

Eden put on her no-nonsense voice. 'I'll be back on Tuesday. And, Tracey…' she smiled '…thanks.'

As soon as she set the receiver down her cell phone rang out. She pushed up, dug into her purse, which she'd left on the kitchen counter, and checked the number.

Sabrina?

Her pulse rate flipping out, Eden thumbed the green key. 'What's wrong?'

'Nothing's wrong,' Sabrina said, in a calming tone. 'I just wanted to talk to you before tomorrow.'

Eden released the breath she'd been holding.

From an early age, their mother as well as their father had left for work before the girls caught the bus for school. Eden had been entrusted to do Sabrina's hair, make her lunch. She'd felt more like Sabrina's second mother than a sister. She'd moved from hometown Gosford to the city at age eighteen and Sabrina had followed when she'd begun college too.

Now Eden's little chick was all grown and leaving the nest. And, irrespective of her maternal instincts for Sabrina and her misgivings about Nathan, Eden had better quit acting like a nineteenth-century chaperone or she'd risk pushing Sabrina away. If Sabrina ever needed her, Eden wanted her to know she would always be there. Everyone made mistakes, herself included.

'I was wrong to behave the way I did,' Eden confessed now. Not only spouting off this afternoon in the hotel suite, but also for asking to meet Devlin to speak with Nathan, not that Sabrina would ever hear about that. 'Of course you have a right to make you own decisions. And I support you.'

She was glad she sounded sincere. She meant what she'd said and intended to stand by her words, no matter how much it pained her to think of her sister's feelings being crushed.

Eden imagined Sabrina's heartened smile. 'Thanks, Ee. That means a lot—to both of us.' A brief pause. 'Is Devlin there?'

'No.'

'Oh.' Sabrina sounded surprised. 'We were hoping…'

Eden's mouth curved on a suspicious grin. 'Hoping what?'

'We didn't set it up for you and Devlin to be alone to hatch anything, honest. But when we had to go out, we got to talking and Nate said wouldn't it be cool if you two got together again? I could've fallen over when Devlin came striding out of that room today.'

Eden crossed a single arm over the curling sensation in her belly. At least Sabrina didn't sound offended, more amused. But she had it wrong.

'We're not getting back together, if that's what you think.'

'Really?' Sabrina didn't sound convinced.

'What happened in that suite was a one-off.' But that was a lie. 'Well…pretty much a one-off,' she muttered.

'Now you're really confusing me.'

Eden pinched the bridge of her nose and exhaled. Oh, she might as well come clean. The truth would get out anyway and the revelation would sit better coming from her.

'I won't be here tomorrow when you collect your things. I'm going away for a couple of days.'

'With Devlin?' Sabrina squeaked, then called out, 'Nate, she's going away with Devlin!' Back into the mouthpiece, 'I'm so happy for you.'

She tried to deflect the ricocheted sense of excitement. 'Don't be. It's not what you think.'

'I think you're still in love with him.'

Eden shut her eyes and focused.

She would not even entertain the suggestion. She'd spent too long coaching herself *not* to be in love with Devlin. Besides, he'd never been truly serious about her. He was a consummate bachelor who valued his freedom. This two-day escape was simply something they both needed to do and never do again.

But there were some things she didn't need to explain to her sister, particularly when she was having trouble making sense of them herself.

'We'll talk next week,' she told Sabrina. After she'd moved in with Nathan.

'Okay. Love you, Ee.'

Eden smiled softly. 'Love you too.'

As soon as Eden disconnected her cell phone buzzed again. She answered without checking the display. 'Eden here.'

'Have you made that phone call?'

Her hand went to her lurching heart. 'Devlin?'

'I wanted to say goodnight, sleep well.'

'You did?' she murmured, her hand travelling to her throat, which had tightened with emotion.

'I'll see you tomorrow. Nine a.m. sharp.'

He disconnected without getting her response, which was a good thing. She mightn't have been able to speak over the bittersweet ache in her chest.

This was all too familiar—too touching—which meant bubbles of happiness mixed with painful splinters of doubt.

She gazed at the phone for a long moment, then crossed to her desk and trailed her hand over her latest pastel-pink diary, the year embossed in gold on its cover.

Eden's twelfth birthday present from her favourite aunt had been a diary, and she'd penned entries practically every day since. Nowadays lots of people used blogs, which was a great new twist on a classic tradition. But she preferred to transpose her truest personal thoughts on actual rather than virtual pages. Having something to physically hold and flip through brought the memories that much closer.

Now she pulled out a bottom drawer and retrieved a diary from three years ago and opened to a favourite page.

Devlin took me to the movies tonight. Afterward we had supper and talked lots before he saw me to my door. He'd only been gone a few minutes when he rang, wanting to say a second goodnight and sleep tight. He's such a gentleman...but he kisses like a bad boy.

I think I'm falling in love.

CHAPTER SEVEN

AT NINE THIRTY the next morning, with Devlin standing beside her, Eden stammered, coughed and finally choked the words out.

'You want me to jump into *that*?'

At nine o'clock, as promised, Devlin had knocked on her door. After riding her apartment-building lift, they'd slid into the luxurious interior of his Lexus coupé. Her stomach muscles knotting, she'd silently gone over the belongings she'd packed while he'd praised the fine weather and conveyed that he'd lined up a subordinate so he'd be free the next day.

Eden had swallowed the ball of nerves bunched in her throat and consciously relaxed her stranglehold on the seat belt. She'd come this far. No turning back. No matter what.

Yet standing here now, she realised that the fiend Devlin Stone had lulled her into a false sense of semi-security only to drive them to her personal hangman's noose.

An airport.

On the tarmac beside her, he pushed the mirrored aviator glasses closer to the bridge of his nose and, with an admiring angle to his jaw, inspected the aircraft's compact lines.

'It's a Cessna 152. A few years old now, but that's part of her charm. She's a gorgeous lady to fly.'

Barely hearing a word—the rush of blood pounding in her ears was too loud—Eden swallowed over the convulsing muscles in her throat. Someone might've stolen her kneecaps, she felt so unsteady and weak. She'd been prepared to face this challenge of staying with Devlin for two days head-on. She'd been determined to be brave.

But not *this* brave.

She forced her rubbery lips to move. 'Y-you didn't mention we'd be *flying* anywhere.'

Sliding his glasses off, he studied her. 'I thought you'd conquered your fear of planes.'

'As in *big* planes. Really big planes. And even then I'm queasy.'

'Little planes are the same as big planes, only smaller.' A palm on her back, he urged her forward. 'I personally vouch for your safety. I won't be surprised if you enjoy it.'

'As much as you'd enjoy wearing a skirt and singing "Pop Goes My Heart" on the Opera House stairs.'

He laughed. 'You wish.' He prodded her again and, although her heels dug in, they inched forward. 'I've had my pilot's licence going on five years. You're perfectly safe. We have more chance of crashing a car.'

'But without the added bonus of spiralling to earth at a thousand miles per hour.'

He refitted his glasses and lowered his voice. 'If you feel that strongly...'

'Do you have parachutes?'

As soon as it was out she wanted to swallow the words back down. No way would she cramp up inside that nutshell with wings, parachute or not.

His mouth twitched. 'Would it really make a difference?'

Her upper lip felt cool with perspiration while her brow was hot enough to burn. Tiny chills were racing up and down her spine. In a word, she was terrified, but she was more terrified about backing out of this trip. She *had* to do this. Finally get Devlin Stone out of her system. Lying in bed last night, staring at the ceiling, she'd coined a new personal motto.

Do Devlin or die.

She hadn't meant literally.

Heart belting against her ribcage, she clutched her over-nighter under her chin and forced one foot forward. Then the other. When he stood back, hands on hips, a big grin on his handsome face, she manufactured a scowl.

'What are you waiting for? A ticker-tape parade?'

His smile turned warm. 'You deserve one.'

They climbed on board. The interior smelled much like an older model car left in the sun. He took a seat at the front and indicated she should sit beside him. Her gaze zig-zagged over the maze of instruments on the dashboard. Looked like a heck of a lot of things could go wrong.

'Might make you feel better if I explain what these all do?' He pointed to a clock device. 'This is the—'

Her sweaty palm death-gripped his thigh. 'Please. Don't.' With the small cabin squeezing in more around her, her teeth were a bee's knee away from chattering. 'I only have one question.'

His eyes shone with admiration. 'What's that?'

'Do you have paper bags?'

'Panic attack?'

She showed him an index finger and thumb an inch apart. 'An iddy-biddy bit of a one.'

'There's only one cure for that.'

'Morphine?'

'To get this baby in the air. Buckle up.' His chest beneath the polo shirt inflated as he fastened his belt. 'We'll be there in no time.' He indicated her headphones and fixed his own. 'We'll talk to keep your mind off the altitude.'

He fired the single engine, the noise kicked in, then he did his thing with the instruments. With her seat vibrating beneath her, she closed her eyes, said a prayer and didn't breathe again until the plane was in the air.

A petrifying yet strangely exhilarating ten thousand feet in the air.

After the initial 'I'm gonna throw up' reflex had passed, Eden was beyond amazed to learn that Devlin had been right. When she convinced herself it was too late to back out and forced her mind into a rickety state of acceptance, she chanced a stiff look out the window and, remarkably, began to enjoy the ride.

After passing patchworks of suburban buildings and swimming pools, they flew over a field of low stratus cloud. On the right an endless stretch of tranquil teal ocean glittered with sun diamonds.

Man, she was really doing it! It was worth the half-moons dug into the palms of her hands—this sense of freedom and daring, knowing that, if the sun failed to rise tomorrow, she'd faced her greatest fear and could face it again.

Sorry truth was she'd *have* to if she wanted to get back home.

Devlin pointed out landmarks—the snaking Hawkesbury River, the shipping port town of Newcastle, the peaks and valleys of the Great Dividing Range, the fourth longest mountain range in the world. She'd got close to comfortable with hurtling through the stratosphere in a tin can by the time the plane began to descend—then the knot in her freefalling stomach wrenched again.

Holding her headphones, she stole a wide-eyed glance straight down. No land beneath them, only water—and more water.

Her thin laugh held a hysterical edge. 'I didn't think this was a seaplane.'

He pointed and she heard through the headphones, 'There's our destination.'

Eden sat forward and focused. 'An island.'

'It's called *le Paradis sur Terre*. It means heaven on earth.'

A few minutes later, the plane touched down and the brakes were applied. As the engine and wind noise changed pitch again the cabin bumped and she clamped her eyes shut, clinging on for dear life. When the plane rolled to a stop, she told her heart to quit booming, then cautiously opened her eyes.

Beyond the window, majestic palms bordered the unsealed airstrip. Sprays of vermillion, deepest scarlet, sun-kissed orange—a veritable painter's palette of flowers wove natural tapestries throughout the lush foliage. When they emerged from the craft and stepped into the warm luminous sunshine, Eden was lifted up by the sweet fresh air—the scent of sea blended with the perfume of exotic plants.

Amazed, she rotated three-sixty degrees. 'Is this place real? It's not a set for a remake of *Endless Love*?'

His dark blue eyes sparkling, he ruffled a hand through hair flattened by the headphones. 'It's real. Come and meet the staff.'

So engrossed by the scenery, she hadn't noticed a man

and woman walking towards them. Middle-aged, the man wore dungarees and a broad welcoming smile beneath his wide-brimmed straw hat. The woman's pink-and-yellow sarong was tied at the nape. Her hair was long, uncommonly thick and dark. Her eyes were as gentle as a doe's.

Eden liked them both instantly.

The man extended his large tanned hand. 'This is Tianne. And I'm Gregory.' His voice was deep and clear like the coral-laced waters surrounding the island. 'You must be Mr Stone.'

'Call me Devlin.' He tipped his head. 'This is Eden.'

'Such a pretty name.' Tianne presented a bunch of vibrant flowers that smelled like jasmine. 'I hope you enjoy your stay.'

Eden accepted the gift. 'I'm sure I will.'

Gregory removed his hat. 'Mr Bruce asked us to have every convenience on hand. The cold box is full. The wine rack too. There's a map in the bungalow pointing out the island's many wonders.'

Scanning the scene, pleased with what he saw and heard, Devlin nodded. 'Excellent. We'll see you back here on Tuesday, then.'

'You'll hear our boat's motors returning after dawn. There's a second boat moored and fuelled if you want to reach parts of the island that way.'

Gregory explained the short route to their accommodation, as well as to the staff quarters a short distance away. Then Tianne gently waved her palms in overlapping figure eights. 'Pleasant stay.'

With knapsacks on their backs, the couple disappeared through a track in the foliage.

'It's a reasonably short trip by motorboat to the mainland,' Devlin explained as he relieved her of her over-nighter then, looping his arm through hers, steered her towards the track Gregory had indicated.

Eden held onto his arm and once again took in their fantastical surrounds. 'Then we're all alone?'

'Just you, me—' he chuckled '—and a million birds.'

At the same time they heard Tianne and Gregory's boat engine kick in and the craft speed away, a gorgeous Balinese-style dwelling with a thatched roof appeared in a clearing. The design fitted perfectly with the tropical setting, exuding understated luxury as well as sturdy authenticity.

He led her up three wide timber steps. 'You like?'

'Are you kidding?' She *loved* it. 'Gregory mentioned a Mr Bruce. He owns this island?' Devlin nodded. 'What is he? A bazillionaire?'

'Pretty much,' he said matter-of-factly. 'R. J. Bruce and I hit it off at a private poker game in London. He said if I ever wanted to visit *le Paradis* to give him a call. He comes here maybe twice a year.'

Eden soaked up her surroundings…the sweet sound of the birds, the ideal temperature, the spicy calming scent of virgin nature. 'If I were Mr Bruce, I don't know I'd ever want to leave.'

On the veranda, Devlin turned and studied her as she stood on a lower step. 'We can stay longer if you'd like.'

His eyes looked so deep, she wanted to fall into them and never come up for air. But this adventure needed a finite time frame or, once again, she'd be confronting the problem of kicking her Devlin habit.

So, before she could become any more tempted, she threw back her shoulders and reminded him, 'We both have responsibilities to get back to.'

She passed him, walking through into the main room. She gasped when she caught sight of a magnificent spread of food on an enormous low square table.

She drifted forward. 'What's all this?'

Exotic fruit, every colour, every shape, and a pitcher of some exquisite-smelling nectar—mango and perhaps passionfruit based—sat on a bamboo place mat.

Feeling like an island princess, she snapped off a plump green grape, sighing when the juice burst in her mouth at the same time she saw the view from the bedroom.

Classic Oriental furniture looked to be crafted from the darkest wood. Abstract sculptures of tall, slender animals and birds presided in a serene and regal fashion around the room. A porcelain bowl and pitcher sat on the dresser while a motorised fan, consisting of three large rattan flaps on a rod, washed fresh air back and forth.

The bed wasn't king-sized. Rather it looked…cosy. Piles of pillows and cushions, so many shapes of sequined coloured silk, were piled up against the heavy wooden bed head.

Drawn by the view, she crossed the room.

Through the large window—free of glass—scallops of Pacific Ocean surf crashed and ebbed upon an idyllic stretch of beach. Seagulls wheeled beneath a dome of blemish-free blue while stranded seashells sparkled on the sand.

A set of strong arms wrapped around her from behind. Her stomach jumped and she tried to spin around, but Devlin held her in place.

'What's the verdict?' he asked against her ear as his hands folded over her waist and drew her closer still.

With his fresh masculine scent mingling with the salty air, she sighed again and leaned her head back against his shoulder. 'It's enough to make me want to move from the city.'

'What? No mochachinos, no theatre, no shoe stores.'

'Just the ocean, the sun—'

'And you and me.'

Her heart thudded madly as he twirled her around. His smiling eyes roamed her face as his hands shaped down her bare arms.

'What do you want to do?'

She longed to be brazen and suggest they jump into that bed and do what they both ached to do. Already she felt his hot, hard body moving over hers, heard his rumbling endearments as he brought her to the cusp of a mind-blowing orgasm.

But while she'd felt beyond reckless and impatient yesterday when she'd suggested they get a room, now the tingly wash through her veins urged her to squeeze as much out of this experience as she could.

Initially two days alone with Devlin had seemed like an eternity that held far too many uncertainties, yet, now they were here, time seemed to be turned on its head, falling through the hourglass way too quickly. If her heart could handle this limited spell in his company, she might as well prolong and savour every delectable minute.

His eyes burned into hers, waiting for a verdict, while the island hummed of a thousand exotic, and erotic, possibilities.

'Late yesterday you were interested in talking,' she said, drawing out his suspense.

'We talked on the plane.' Edging closer, his head slanted near to hers. 'I'm practically talked out.'

'And now you're ready for something more.'

His hot gaze on her lips, his fingers brushed her cheek as he combed back a strand of her hair. 'More sounds good.'

'Like getting out of these travel clothes?'

'A sensible idea.'

'And maybe we should grab a bottle of chilled champagne and some fruit.'

'I'm tempted.' His lips hovered achingly close to hers. 'More than tempted.'

'We can have a picnic.'

He grinned. 'In bed.'

'Outdoors.'

His smile changed, then his hand wove around to caress the responsive dip low in her back. 'Outdoors definitely works for me.'

Her fingertips measured his sandpaper jaw. 'We could go for a swim afterwards. I brought my bikini.'

'Glad you came prepared, but—' he flicked open the top button on her blouse '—you won't need it.'

Twenty minutes later, he and Eden were indeed outdoors, enjoying a meal of cheese, airy bread, the freshest fruit along with that nectar, which had been brewed for the pleasure of the gods.

Lounging on his side on a blanket brought from the bungalow, Devlin lifted the pitcher. 'More?'

Eden presented her goblet. 'I know the note Tianne left said this doesn't contain alcohol but doesn't it taste like a cross between a fruity Cosmopolitan and sarsaparilla?'

'I'd have said cognac and ginger beer.'

Her brow furrowed—*no way*. 'Whatever it is, it's heavenly.'

She enjoyed a long sip then, setting her goblet aside, laid back, one arm behind her head as she gazed dreamily up at flawless blue visible between the bobbing palm fronds. Unaware of his study of the delicate shape of her brows, the tantalising tilt of her nose, she reached blindly for the plate. Her hand landed on a peach. She took a leisurely bite and chewed before her arm fell like a weight back onto the blanket.

'I feel too lazy for a swim,' she murmured.

He craned forward and angled his head to drop a lingering kiss on her inside wrist. 'You lie there and relax.'

'What will you do?'

His mouth cruised a little higher. 'I'll keep myself entertained.'

'Does your entertainment include getting me out of this bikini?'

He pressed a meaningful kiss on her shoulder. 'You'd better believe it.'

Back at the bungalow, when he'd suggested they forgo swimsuits, she'd wound out of his embrace and playfully insisted. Seemed she'd found some perspective and had lowered yesterday's bravado down a gear. Which was fine by him. Uncontrollable passion had its place, but he'd take 'slow burn' to 'wham-bam' any day.

What was more, if he'd relented and signed for a room yesterday, she'd have found it too easy to shoot through after the event, which he suspected would've been her plan. And that wouldn't do, either.

Which meant what? he wondered as his attentive gaze slid from her smooth neck along her arm to the peach juice trickling down her fingers, pooling in her palm.

Did he want to continue seeing Eden?

But that wasn't the question, he countered, skimming his lips over her creamy shoulder again. He hadn't been the one to call it quits three years ago. The sticking point had been the spectre of a wedding hovering over his head.

Given her retort yesterday—the one hurled at Sabrina about not seeing a ring on her finger—pinning down a man was still an issue for Eden.

One day in the distant future he would tie the knot, have a family—but it would need to be with the concrete knowledge that when he said 'I do', it would be for ever. He wouldn't be corralled into that kind of commitment, or lose his head and jump in ahead of time. If nothing else, dear ol' dad's ambivalence towards his family had taught his son the pitfalls of that mistake.

Eden set aside her peach and propped up on her elbows to study the crystal-blue lake. They'd thought about visiting the beach and surf, but this inland tropical canopy was a cooler proposition. In a strange way, it was more private too, if that were possible.

She shielded her eyes, her gaze wandered to the left and her face lit up. 'Look at the amazing patterns on that cliff.'

The craggy face presented a jigsaw of dark crevices carved over the eons. A gentle stream cascaded over the lip, spilling a crystalline veil of water that poured into and became one with the lake.

She joked, 'Looks like a good challenge for you.'

'For climbing?'

'Wanna try?'

'I'm not in the mood for physical exertion.'

Not that kind, anyway.

She crunched up and hugged her legs, her cheek resting on her knees as she arched an eyebrow at him. 'Then I'll have to do it without you.'

About to run his lips down her outside leg, he coughed out, *'You?'*

'Yeah. *Me.*'

'I vote for a splash around that waterfall instead.'

'We can do both.'

Oh, come on. 'No way are you interested in scaling slimy rocks.'

She released her knees. 'I don't know if I am or not. I've never tried. I didn't think I'd enjoy the plane ride either.'

He blinked twice. Was she for real?

'If you're interested,' he said carefully, 'I can organise some beginner lessons.'

She sat up straighter. 'I could have my first lesson here. If I fall I'll only hit water.'

Unease scuttled over his skin. He didn't like that look in her eye. A look that said, *You can't stop me.*

'We don't know how deep the water is,' he said, wondering if she'd had one sip of that mysterious nectar too many.

She inspected the cliff, the water, and nodded. 'Good point.'

No word of warning. She simply sprang up and shallow dived into the water. He'd never seen her move so fast!

By the time he found his feet, she'd freestyled out to the waterfall and plunged into the drink like a duck after its dinner. Legs braced, senses on alert, Devlin waited for her to re-emerge. A few seconds of his pulse thudding at his temples and he strode into water up to his thighs, scanning the surface where she'd disappeared with an eagle eye.

When more time passed, he cursed, filled his lungs and prepared to dive. But then Eden broke the water's surface as if she'd been shot from a cannon.

Gasping for air, she combed back her hair, then waved and called out, 'It's plenty deep enough.'

As relief fell through his centre he scowled more than laughed. 'I'll give you *deep enough.*'

He dived in and, on reaching her, roped an arm around her waist. He side-stroked through the waterfall, grinning at her struggle, which was about as convincing as a rag doll's. The cool stream cascaded over their heads until they broke through the fall and he plonked Eden's smarty pants on the moss-covered rock ledge.

While sheets of rushing water curtained off the outside world, the smell of moss and fern lingered within a space that bounced muffled echoes off its concave wall. Snug. A lot like yesterday's hideaway when the rain had pinned them in. The big difference today was Eden's disposition, which was buoyant, to say the least.

He shook excess water from his hair, wet-dog style, then, hands on the ledge, pushed up and out of the water to sit beside her.

'Now,' he growled, leaning towards her, 'about that bikini…'

She tipped away. 'You'll have to catch me first.'

Flipping over onto all fours, she scrambled off. But he grabbed her bikini bottom before she could escape, his fingers curling into the flimsy back band. Unprepared for her abrupt change in momentum, her top half continued to advance while her lower half got left behind. She fell forward on her belly and the bottoms came down. Shrieking, she flipped over, one hand flying to cover the exposed juncture of her legs.

He laughed and reminded her, 'A little late for that kind of modesty.'

Her eyes narrowed even while they danced. 'You don't play fair.'

'I play to win.'

He grabbed the gusset of the bikini pants, which were

caught at her knees, and whipped them off past her shins and feet. Enjoying her teasing mood and their game, he somehow managed to realign his focus from her lower regions to her bikini top and the perfect pebbled breasts rising and falling beneath the bright yellow triangles.

Their game was about to get serious.

He absently cast the bottoms aside. 'I'd ask you to take that off—' his chin tipped at her top as he bent forward '—but I'm looking forward to doing it myself.'

'Good luck!'

In a fluid movement, she snatched the bottoms off the rock and rolled into the water. He missed catching her by a millimetre. Loving the energy thundering through his blood, he plunged into the water after her.

When Devlin surfaced on the other side of the water-fall, he threw a glance around. Eden didn't appear to be in the lake, or on the blanket on the sand.

'Eden?' Treading water, he spun around, then spun around again. 'Eden! Where are you?'

'Up here!'

His attention shot to the cliffs and he almost swallowed his tongue. Her bikini bottoms were in place, which he'd half expected. He hadn't expected to see her clinging to the side of that rock face, not far up, but far enough to hurt herself if she fell and clipped the side.

This behaviour wasn't normal. Not for Eden, in any case. What the heck was in that nectar?

'Eden,' he said in a low calm tone, 'get down from there—*slowly*.'

'It's deep enough if I fall.'

'You're not used to climbing,' he said levelly. 'You'll hurt yourself.'

Hesitation flickered over her face, then she peered down. Immediately unsteady, she clutched at the rock again.

She grinned weakly. 'It looks higher up here than I thought.'

He pointed at her, willing his finger to keep her feet glued to the spot. 'Stay put. I'll come up and get you.'

She shook her head as if he were bullying her. 'I don't need rescuing, Devlin. I got myself up here. I'm more than capable of getting myself down.'

Before he could object, she raised her arms, closed her eyes—perhaps to say a prayer—then executed a perfect swan dive into the lake.

Letting loose a string of expletives, he waited until she popped up for air. Then he captured her and swam towards the bank. She was laughing and coughing when he dumped her on the blanket.

Flopping back, she sighed at the sky. 'That was *fun*.'

Standing over her, he set his palms on his knees and got his breath. 'No. That was stupid.'

'Because I did it and you didn't? I thought you'd approve of my impulsiveness.'

'Why the hell would I—'

But then he stopped, sized her up and smiled a knowing smile.

This was payback. He'd scared her three years ago when that ship in Scotland had capsized. She'd wanted to give him a taste of his own medicine. He couldn't believe she'd pull such a stunt. One part of him wanted to applaud her sense of adventure. A bigger part wanted to throw her over his knee and spank her soundly so she wouldn't try it again.

Which was ludicrous.

He wasn't her keeper.

Just as she wasn't his.

Breathless, she sat up a little unsteadily, a big grin on her face. 'I'm not tired any more.'

Setting his jaw, he snatched up the picnic basket. 'Then we'll pack up and head back.' Before any more delinquent schemes hatched in her head. 'You've had enough sun.'

'Sunbathing wasn't what I had in mind.'

She reached around and pulled the bow at her back then unceremoniously flipped the yellow triangles up over her head.

As if steel pins had been removed from his legs, Devlin fell onto his knees. Drinking in the voluptuous lines of her divine form, he tried again to make sense of her spontaneity. When he analysed the teasing promise in her eyes, another cog clicked into place.

With a wry grin, he shoved the basket aside. 'You want to drive me completely insane.'

Tease him until he begged for mercy.

She held out her arm to him. 'Is it working?'

He lowered over her until, curling back, she lay, trapped, beneath him.

He growled against her lips, 'I'll let you be the judge.'

CHAPTER EIGHT

When Eden's eyes widened then blinked up at him, Devlin stiffened and, by some miracle, held off from covering her mouth with his.

She seemed to be holding her breath. Going over something in her mind. He'd done all the thinking he needed to do. Time for *action*. Time to have each other fully, no excuses, no holding back. After her performance just now after he'd dragged her out of the water, she *had* to want the same.

So why was she peering up at him as if she had second thoughts?

'Can I offer a suggestion?' she asked sheepishly.

Devlin's jaw shifted.

He liked foreplay and games as much as the next guy, but he certainly hoped this wasn't a ploy to wiggle out and run away from him again. This tug of war had gone on for twenty-four hours. Whenever one was ready to proceed, the other had found some reason to delay the inevitable.

She'd consented to come away with him, had flirted with him. As of this minute she lay beneath him, her breasts rubbing, with each breath, against his bare chest. There wasn't another living soul within miles and he was so worked up, his every thought was trained against the urge to fall back upon caveman instincts, which meant ignoring her question and taking his pleasure while he kissed her senseless.

Thankfully sanity prevailed.

With his erection strained against his trunks and her belly, his response came out a husky growl. 'What's your suggestion?'

No words. Rather she slid her damp palms between them and gave his chest a token push. His every muscle locked as his brow lowered and his temperature crept up the scale.

Had he misread her? Maybe he'd overestimated that kiss in the rain, her uninhibited response in that steamy room yesterday. But what about her frolicking in the water a moment ago?

Damnation, did she intend to make love with him or not?

While his darkening gaze flickered over her beautiful face, her golden hair swept back from their swim, his mouth instinctively lowered again, so close her ragged breath stirred over his lips, as if begging him to read her 'stop' as a 'please proceed'.

And he'd better pull back now while he still had the strength.

Unable to hide his frustration and doubt, he pushed up onto his knees. Taking her time, Eden repositioned up onto her haunches too. Face to face, she looked squarely into his eyes, then cupped and lifted his jaw. Lightly—carefully— she kissed the hot beating hollow at the base of his throat.

A swirling backdraft of desire blasted through to his core. The sensation was so swift, so strong, he felt compelled to warn her if she was playing again, she was playing with a fire that was perilously close to raging out of control.

But before he could force the words up over the mind-drugging tightness low in his gut, her mouth touched him again, her soft cool lips first caressing his left collarbone then the right, her enticing touch grazing over the crisp hair on his chest, her kiss nipping at a nipple, before trailing further down his centre, her fingers trailing behind.

His head rocked back and his eyes drifted closed as he surrendered to this to-die-for sensation.

Oh, yes, *this* was his Eden.

When her hand scooped into the front of his swimming trunks and freed his raging erection, he clenched his hands by his sides and ground out, *For God's sake*, 'Don't stop.'

Her tongue ran a lazy line around his navel before she answered, 'Not even if the sky cracked wide open and fell in.'

She stroked then squeezed his length until the groan of exquisite pleasure rumbling in his chest escaped his throat. In response, she scooped lower and kneaded that part of him that was bunched tight enough to explode.

When her mouth skimmed down and her tongue slipped around his burning tip, his erection jumped and every hair on his body stood up. With her lips slipping over the top of him, she angled her head and went down while her hand in his trunks rubbed and caressed.

His spine arched back as he glowed with the scorching, wonderful need to detonate. Unable to resist, his palm shaped the back of her damp hair, encouraging her to take more of him, which she did with exquisite skill. When her teeth skimmed back up, a tingling wave of darkest pleasure ran up his legs, pushing fast, pushing hard.

Silently cursing, he bunched every muscle in his body, found her jaw and, drawing her back, willed her to meet his eyes.

'I'd like you to do that all day—' he swallowed '—but I'm not sure I'm strong enough.'

Her parted lips glistened as her fingers fanned over his groin. 'Let's see how strong you are.'

She drew him into her mouth again. When her tongue looped round and round, his body shook against the urge to be done with it and have his release this way. He knew she wouldn't object.

But he wanted to bring her to the same state of finely balanced madness that he battled now. He wanted her to know the almost painful ecstasy shooting like a blowtorch through his veins. And he wanted to bring her to that point without using his hands or his mouth.

He found the will power to draw her away and urge her up. Holding her chin, he kissed her deeply, letting her know how much he enjoyed, and had missed, the things she did with him. His mouth covering hers, his hand skied down her throat to find and sculpt one heavy breast, then roll and pluck the sensitive bead until she whimpered against his lips.

'Keep doing that, and I won't be responsible for my actions.' She shivered against him as if to show him just how serious she was.

An arm looping around to support her back, he lay her down on the blanket. He blindly swept the plate and goblets aside, then, kneeling between her legs, he swiftly removed her bikini briefs before he nudged her thighs wider apart with his knees.

He skimmed two fingers between her silky folds. She was so wet and welcoming—the sight of her, the scent, was almost enough to make him forget his manners and succumb to that inner beast still clamouring to break free.

Instead he drew a slick circle with his finger precisely where and exactly how she liked it.

She bucked at his knowing touch and held his hand, pressing against the spot.

Lowering over her, he whispered against her flushed cheek, 'Not yet. Not yet.'

Her eyes shut, she sighed out a quivering breath and nodded.

Tenderly pressing a kiss to one side of her mouth, he opened her with his fingers then pushed slowly in, stopping only when she arched luxuriously beneath him and he knew he'd filled her as much as this initial connection allowed.

The breath left her body as she quivered and held onto his shoulders. 'Don't move. Stay just like that.'

He grinned. 'You mean like this?'

Almost imperceptibly, he ground against her body, shifting his hips.

An intense yet blissful smile curved her lips. 'Yes, *exactly* like that.' Her fingertips feathered the span that joined his shoulders to neck. 'You're enjoying this, aren't you? Teasing me. Making me want you more.'

He murmured against her brow, 'Ask me something hard.'

She grinned wickedly. 'Count backwards from ten.'

When her inner muscles contracted—pulling him in, holding him tight—a fine film of sweat broke down the indentation of his back, on his brow. He hissed in air, groaning at the powerful sensation before playfully shaking his brain.

'So what comes after nine?'

When her sultry laugh escaped, he hardened more and his primitive brain took over the synapses that made him a man first and last. Relishing the moment, he began to move.

Her legs coiled around his thighs and her head dropped one side, her face a fascinating study in sheer ecstasy.

'Oh, Devlin, I've missed this.'

He turned her head back and stole a deliberate, penetrating kiss. He wanted her, all of her. And, yes, he'd missed her too. So much.

Already treading a razor's edge—already so close to that peak—he drove inside her, savouring her writhing, impassioned response.

'Say it again,' he murmured close to her ear.

Say you missed me. Say you want more.

And she did, but not with words.

His next kiss swallowed the mewling sound leaking from her throat as her calves pushed him in and her body grew taut then contracted around him. His heart pounding, he reached down to cup her bottom, pushing her closer as pinpoints of light tingled and built in his head and his blood.

He groaned against the vital burn, and a heartbeat later was flung into the grip of a heavenly, hammering high. So elemental and raw. So exquisite and adored.

He'd sell his soul to never come down.

When they returned to the bungalow late in the day, Eden couldn't help but beam at the feeling of walking on air. Walking on clouds.

In the west a huge orange ball sank into its fiery horizon, casting a jewelled glow over the leaves, the sand and, beyond the island, a shimmering net on the shadowy sea. A symphony of lively cricket song filled the air, and as they traipsed up the stairs she wrapped her arms more securely around Devlin, resting her cheek against his chest while he held her near.

Held her as if she belonged there.

Same way this day belonged in her dreams, she thought, climbing the last step and holding him tighter. How many hours had she spent locked in and around Devlin's soul-lifting embrace this afternoon? An embrace that, before yesterday, she'd given up hope of knowing again. If only she could hold onto this magic and tie these wings to her feet for ever.

But, of course, that was impossible.

Just take what you can and be grateful for that.

On the veranda, she stopped and, on a burst of happiness—or was it desperation?—stole a kiss from his raspy jaw.

'I'm going to change for dinner.' Her fingertip wove down the hair on his chest. 'Why don't you pour us some wine?'

A dark brow cocked. 'You don't need more wine.'

After stopping to rethink his statement, she shook her head, no. 'We might've had an opinion on the flavour, but Tianne's note said that nectar wasn't alcohol based.' She rubbed a leisurely hand over one rock-hard pec. 'I feel fine.'

Better than fine.

Trying to smother a grin, he tapped her bottom and they proceeded into the main open-plan room. 'You weren't acting fine earlier.'

He meant her climbing that cliff, removing her top?

'Do you think I did those things because I was intoxicated?'

After he lowered the picnic basket next to a sculpture of an ibis about to take flight, he set his hands low on his hips and shrugged. 'It's the only explanation.'

She laughed. 'So when *you* do out-of-the-ordinary

things, you're feeding an adventurous spirit. When *I* do something wild, I must be drunk.'

He held her shoulders, a sardonic gleam in his eye. 'You'll admit it yourself—you don't like adventure.'

'I'm here, aren't I?' she said silkily.

'Only because you had no choice.' He winced, dropped a kiss on her crown and, after rubbing her shoulders conciliatorily, moved away. 'That came out wrong.'

No offence taken, particularly when she had a prime-time distraction—watching his behind, glorified in those fitting black trunks, as he sauntered away with that leisurely fluid gait she adored.

'You're right,' she admitted freely as her eye-line travelled to the steel girths of his thighs. 'I didn't have a choice in coming here. It was either face my demons, face you, like this, or live in emotional purgatory for the rest of my life.'

Standing at the bar, which was set against a bamboo feature wall, he angled back, his brows mischievously drawn. 'Whoa. That sounds heavy.'

A bit of an exaggeration, she'd concede.

'Thing is, we might not be destined to grow old together, but we do share a chemistry. I needed to see what we started yesterday through to its natural conclusion.'

Simple.

When his jaw shifted and head tilted, her amused laugh slipped out. 'Oh, I'm sorry, Devlin. Am I stealing your thunder?'

But she was only being honest, even if that kind of honesty tarnished this fantasy getaway's glow a smidge.

He lost his pensive look and dropped onto his haunches to select wine from the lower rack.

'I'm merely trying to get this straight,' he said, his finger running over the labels. 'This time away, as far as you're concerned, is purely about sex?'

She crossed her arms and grinned. Trust a man to reduce it to that. And was he truly having such a hard time finding the right wine or was he keeping his gaze averted so she couldn't read the relief and glee in his eyes?

'This time away is about having fun,' she explained. 'About letting go.' *Then letting go once and for all.* 'No one should have to tiptoe around pretending it's anything more than that.'

His broad back to her, he didn't answer—only rose to his full height and set the selected wine on the bar ledge. Content to watch the musculature of his shoulders and back work in perfect harmony, she held her tongue while he removed the cap. But when the silence lengthened, icy fingers of dread trickled down her spine.

Maybe she'd gone too far. He was a master of the game, after all, and that meant masking the fundamental reason behind an effective seduction, which masculine vernacular translated into 'getting laid'. Yet her own pride wouldn't let him believe she was that naïve any more. This weekend was what it was. A wonderful time-limited escape.

A relatively safe means to an end.

But if her frankness had dented Devlin's ego, she could always soothe the sting with a dollop of flattery. Getting a bit more off her chest might even do her good.

She wandered towards the ibis, idly shaping a fingertip over the nearest outstretched wing.

'I was nervous when I contacted you about Sabrina and Nathan,' she told him as, with his back to her still, he poured the wine. 'I was close to shaking sitting at that restaurant table, watching you take control of the situation outside, wrenching away that woman's bat, talking with the police. While I pretended to read that menu, one word blinked repeatedly in my mind. Know what that word was?'

He finished pouring. 'I can guess.'

She smiled. Perhaps he could.

'I had good reason to be antsy about seeing you again. It was clear I was still attracted to you. That I needed to see you one last time. I was holding onto the past.' Holding onto bad feelings that had festered too long. Her voice dropped. 'I wasn't very happy with you when we broke up.'

Without facing her, he set the bottle on the timber with a thud. 'You mean after you refused to return my calls.'

'I mean after you callously dismissed my concern for your safety.'

She flinched. She sounded like a martyr. Most unattractive now it had worn so thin.

Finding her calm centre, she moved toward the bedroom and ended on a high note.

'But that's all in the past,' she said, setting a hand on the door jamb. 'And although I have reservations about your brother's true intentions towards Sabrina,' she admitted, 'I'm glad I've seen that other side of you.'

Without meeting her gaze, he turned his head fractionally, providing an evocative picture of his classic profile.

'Which side?' he asked.

'The side who cares enough to believe in and stand by someone, rather than closing down and walking off in the other direction.'

He peered at her then over his broad, bronzed shoulder. His tone was sombre, his eyes almost hard.

'Is that the kind of man you think I am?'

Her heart twisted but, given what she knew of him, she could only return a mock-tinged smile.

'Self-awareness really isn't your strong suit.'

Getting back on track, fighting down the regret, she tapped the door jamb and drew up tall. 'But let's not be morbid. This is two days out of our lives, and I'm happy to say that they're opening up a side of me I never knew existed.'

'Never knew existed,' he clarified, collecting the wine glasses and prowling towards her, 'or kept locked away?'

She blinked. That didn't make sense.

'You said yourself I've never been the adventurous type.'

'What was that about self-awareness and strong suits?'

When he stopped before her, her skin heated at the deliberate challenge in his gaze. A challenge she had no intention of tackling now.

This conversation was over. They needed to get back to that other place, the easy, *fun* place they'd shared by that lake. She had one more beautiful day coming to her, as well as two scintillating nights. And, come hell or high water, she was going to enjoy them. And that meant sharing her body with Devlin without letting him see any more of her heart.

She curved her lips into a light smile. 'Keep that glass safe for me. I'll be back out soon.'

She closed the shutter doors and stood behind them for a long moment allowing her warmed flesh to cool, her tripping heartbeat to wind down. Then, with renewed vigour and determination, she headed for her overnighter, which sat in a corner of the room.

Tonight she'd wear a silk-sheen georgette scoop-necked flapper dress, her only accessories matching chandelier earrings and a smear of warm red lipstick. Stylish yet casual with an emphasis on *fun*.

No more talk about self-awareness, she vowed, kicking off her sandals. She'd done enough soul searching. Starting yesterday it was the year of no regrets. She'd said what she had to say. Even felt better for it. But her 'sharing' just now was meant to make up for her calling a spade a spade. She wouldn't let her recollection of her deeper feelings change the mood of the time they had left.

Halfway to her bag, her step faltered and her gaze skirted across to the bed.

On the burnished silk spread lay a dusky pink evening gown, fitting from bodice to hip before the cut flowed out into a skirt as light and delicate as gossamer. Drifting nearer, she saw the dress straps, above a square neckline, were made up of delicate rosettes. The skirt's twin splits travelled either side of the centre front and didn't stop until they hit above the panty line.

Simple, sexy, the ideal shade.

One of the most exquisite gowns she'd ever seen!

Earlier today, when they'd set off on the path that led to the lake, he'd made an excuse to jog back to the bungalow. Guess he'd wanted to set this out. She'd never had anyone do something so romantic. So perfectly thoughtful.

She wanted to race out and bowl him over with a huge thank-you hug for his gift—not of perfume or flowers or jewellery, but something that truly spoke to her. Outstanding fashion, here on a deserted island, of all places.

But such a display would clash with the cool and breezy persona she wanted to convey. She couldn't appear overly emotional. *Vulnerable.* Hopelessly overwhelmed by feelings she'd fought so hard to beat down—

A hot tear slipped down her cheek. Pressing her quivering lips together, she held her hitching breath and swiped the wet away with the back of her hand.

Damn it, she'd thought she'd found a way to fix it, but her heart *still* hurt from missing him all these years. Her soul still ached because he hadn't tried hard enough when she'd refused to return his calls.

The stupid truth was that three years ago she'd wanted him to chase her, to confess how unfair he'd been distancing himself from her, waving off her concern. She'd wanted him to apologise and at last profess his undying love. She'd called his bluff and had lost dismally. The insane part was that, deep down, she'd known she would.

She crumpled onto her knees beside the dress and, with the empty ache in her chest growing, carefully lay her head on the bedspread, looking at the layers of airy fabric, feeling the suffocating lump build more in her throat.

She'd been an idiot—a complete and utter moron kidding herself she could enjoy these days away without repercussions. But, like a kid with a lollipop, she'd just had to have him. And if she hadn't managed it before, how could she possibly forget about him after this? How could she forget his kisses, the graze of his hard, hot body against hers?

Once again she was in danger.

In danger of falling right back in love.

CHAPTER NINE

AFTER Devlin changed into casual trousers and a collared shirt, which he left untucked, he set a match to the half-dozen garden torches then, in the flickering light, waited for his girl out on the veranda. When Eden emerged a few minutes later, he turned from the roll of dark waves crashing on the beach and almost dropped the wine glasses he held.

She looked like a vision. A beautiful, golden-haired, heart-pounding vision.

She glided more than walked across the wooden floor towards him, her face freshly kissed by today's sun, her eyes shining in the scattered torchlight.

'Thanks for the dress.' Stopping before him, she rotated, holding the skirt out so it wafted in the evening breeze. 'It's beautiful.'

He remembered to breathe and inclined his head. 'Glad you like it.'

'It was the perfect surprise.'

'So I'm slowly making up for past offences,' he teased, offering over her wine.

Brow creasing, she dropped her skirt and accepted the glass. 'I'm afraid I said too much earlier—'

'Not at all. I'd rather hear it straight than try to read between your lines.'

'Am I really so cryptic?'

Her tone was gently goading, but her eyes were round, almost pleading, and he suspected her comment might also refer to an earlier time when she'd browsed through a jewellery pamphlet rather than openly broach the subject of diamond rings.

However, given their sombre mood before she'd gone to change, keeping his response relevant but light seemed best.

She wanted fun. He'd give her fun.

He smiled over the rim of his glass. 'Cryptic? A more fitting word might be *teasing*.'

Humour returned to her eyes and her lips curved into a luscious smile. 'Do you mind?'

'Should be more of it.'

'More of this?' She craned up on tiptoe and feathered her lips over the square of his jaw.

He hummed in his throat. 'Much more of that.'

To support his observation, he held her nape and, arching her slightly back, kissed her deeply, his tongue sliding over hers, his respiratory rate spiking at the contact and anticipation of what the coming evening would bring.

When he broke the kiss, she murmured against his lips, 'You're not sick of doing that yet?'

'What a silly question.'

Her eyes sparkled.

When he eased her back up from the dip, she inhaled and looked down at her gown, holding her glass out and twirling again. 'Mind if I ask where you got the dress?'

'I have my contacts.'

She laughed. 'Now who's the tease?'

'I rang a designer friend yesterday,' he confessed, 'after I dropped you off. Tulleau was beside himself when he heard my surprise gift was for none other than the celebrated owner of Temptations.'

'Tulleau? As in the Nicolas Tulleau?'

'I've impressed you.'

'I would *die* to design gowns as recognised as his.'

'You're on your way. I hear you've been nominated for an award this year.'

She shrugged modestly but her blush told him she was pleased that he knew. 'It's great to make the list but I can't see myself winning.'

'You might be pleasantly surprised.'

She merely smiled, then wandered towards the stairs. He followed and when he stood beside her, she asked while gazing up at the heavy full moon, 'What's the one un-achievable thing you'd love to achieve?'

'Besides world peace and the ability to balance a pea on my nose? Let's see. I'd like to race in the Monaco Grand Prix. To feel the power of a Formula One rumbling around me as we hug the turns. I have a friend who's a pit-stop chief and...I'm totally boring you.'

She blinked back from the moon and her thousand-yard stare. 'Not at all.' She cringed. 'Maybe a little. Zooming around the countryside at three hundred kilometres an hour isn't my idea of achieving anything other than hives.' She shrugged. 'Sorry.'

He ran a fingertip down her arm. 'Hey, where's that fun side you showed me earlier?'

'Well, there's fun—' she waggled her brows '—then there's *fun*.'

'I'll have the latter.'

'Sure you can handle it?'

He almost licked his lips. 'Try me.'

She held up a finger—just a minute—and sped off. She returned with a towel and when she floated past him she laid the towel on the middle step before sitting down. With the flowing skirt protected and falling either side and between her exposed long tanned legs, she grabbed a stick off the ground to draw lines in the sand.

When he recognised the grid—noughts and crosses—he clutched at his heart. 'Wait. My blood pressure can't handle the excitement.'

'I read somewhere Formula One cars cost millions to build. This time-honoured pastime, on the other hand, is completely free. I was the champ in fourth grade.'

When she drew a nought in the centre square, he sank down beside her. 'Because you always took the advantage?' Anyone knew whoever went first was destined to win.

She pursed her lips to hide a grin. 'I didn't think you wanted to play?'

'I'm just saying we should've flipped a coin to see who kicked off.'

'Tell you what. If I win this one I'll let you win the next.'

With a fingertip, he marked an X in the top right corner, then sent her a wink. 'Here's a tip. Men don't like to hear "I'll let you win".'

'No kidding,' she deadpanned and put a *hug* below his *kiss*.

'There's something to be said,' he intoned, concentrating on his next move, 'for putting your all into coming first.'

She laughed. 'It's just noughts and crosses.'

He expanded his advice. 'What about that award? Don't you try your best to score sales and build a reputation for your boutique?'

'That's different. That's not a game. It's important.'

He held her eyes with his and, whether it was wise or not, tried to see more…know more.

'Tell me, Eden, what else is important?'

Her gaze and mouth softened. 'Accepting that some things just aren't winnable.'

Then her slim nostrils flared and her gaze fell to the sand. Tossing the stick, she held herself, rubbing her arms as she glanced around. 'It's getting cool, don't you think?'

Clearly she didn't want him to delve deeper into that remark, but he had to wonder who or what was unwinnable. Was she saying he couldn't win her, or she couldn't win him? Maybe she meant their fight to beat their physical attraction for each other was lost. On that point, he'd have to agree.

A sudden cool breeze ruffled the hem of her skirt and he levered himself up. 'I have the perfect remedy to keep us warm.'

He crooked a finger and she accepted his help up. They moved to the centre of the clearing and when he took her in his arms they began to dance to the music of the night birds and palm fronds whispering in the wind.

She rested her cheek against his chest. A few moments passed before she murmured, 'I must say, you do dance well.'

Savouring the feel of her against him again, he brushed his lips over her crown. 'I try.'

'Did you take lessons?'

'It was compulsory before the senior year formal.'

'An exclusive school, no doubt.'

'My father's old stomping ground.'

'You never spoke much about your parents.'

'Didn't I?'

She stiffened at his sullen tone. 'Guess it's a banned subject.'

He set his jaw and peered at a cobalt night sky crowded with stars. 'My father wasn't the nicest of men.'

Startled, she looked up into his face. 'To you?'

'If ignoring your sons can be classed as not nice.'

'Why would he do that?'

He tucked her head back under his chin. 'His biggest regret was getting married.'

He felt the breath leave her body. 'Wow. That must've been hard on your mother.'

Huge understatement.

'Growing up I felt sorry for her,' he explained, 'but my father was such a strong character. She must've seen the writing on the wall. She must have known what kind of man he was.'

'The kind she couldn't win?'

Her subtext this time was clear.

He was the man Eden hadn't won. But what kind of man was that? Someone who believed in and stood by someone he cared about? Or a man who closed down before walking off in the other direction?

A man like his father.

The only thing he was sure about was that he'd mistakenly thought he could get Eden out from under his skin with little more than a kiss. But the more he kissed her, the more he held her, the more he didn't want to let her go.

And that frightened him like nothing else could. He never wanted to hurt Eden as his father had hurt his mother. He didn't want to pursue this relationship if he couldn't fully commit. But when could a man be sure about such things? Was it better to let someone walk rather than expose them to that kind of risk? Eden had already escaped his growing ambivalence once. She'd got too close. He'd put up a wall and had got his space back.

All of it.

In the weeks following their break, he'd decided that was best.

Now he wasn't so sure.

Her cheek against his shirt, she interrupted his thoughts. 'Tomorrow we should have a look at that map Gregory left. We can do some exploring.'

His grip on her hand, on her back, tightened even as he pulled her marginally away.

'I'm not thinking about tomorrow. I want to focus on tonight.'

She blinked slowly. 'Good.'

He narrowed his eyes. What was behind that Mona Lisa smile?

'Why good?' he asked.

'Now that *is* a silly question.'

But as he held her close again, resting his cheek against her silky hair, hearing the dark waves roll upon the beach, he had to wonder just how silly it was.

Was this time away about 'letting go' or discovering what was truly important? Learning what was worth winning.

Worth winning and this time keeping.

Who said that meant getting married?

CHAPTER TEN

THEY didn't eat until almost midnight.

Before that, Eden and Devlin had danced and talked and laughed. Then they'd talked and laughed some more. When they'd been unable to deny the magnetic sizzle arcing between them a moment longer, Devlin had swept her up and, his eyes not leaving hers, carried her to their cosy cushioned bed.

Their love-making was…different. Even better. Was that possible? He helped her out of her gown, then she watched him undress. In nature's quiet, the atmosphere felt almost sacred, as though, if they dared make a joke or spoke above a whisper, the magic would dissipate and, suddenly, they'd be back home.

Perhaps it was only wishful thinking on her part that Devlin felt that way too. Organising and bringing along her beautiful gown was one thing. Being in love all over again— and she was falling in love—was something else entirely.

Yet something dark and foreign in his eyes said he wanted this night to last as much as she did, and beyond the physical…although the physical was way better than good.

When he joined her amongst the pillows and fresh cool sheets, she welcomed him with outstretched arms and unbidden tears edging her eyes. He might have seen them glistening in the moonlight that streaked through the open window. She thought she saw his expression change and his jaw clench before, kneeling over her, he curled an arm around her head and kissed her…kissed her as if all the demons in hell were driving him on.

After they'd made love, they had that picnic in bed. They didn't talk about unwinnable situations, or noughts and crosses or even teasing. They seemed beyond any of that. They'd reached another plane, talking quietly to each other as, outside, the torches one by one flickered and died. And when the smoky mist of early dawn filtered in, Eden tried to stare it down, tried to conjure a spell to will it away.

She wanted the night back. Not tomorrow exploring the island. Not even tomorrow night when they'd share this bed again and their time left together would be whittled down to hours. She definitely didn't want to know about Tuesday morning when they'd hear a motorboat return and would politely relay to Gregory and Tianne what a pleasant time they'd had.

Swallowing against the tears building at the back of her throat, Eden cuddled into the only man meant for her while he ran his fingers lightly up and down her arm and they watched, inch by inch, morning light fill the room.

Felt, minute by minute, their time slip away.

When Eden woke, Devlin lay on his side facing away from her.

Her throat ached at the magnificent sight of him…his broad back moving with the steady rhythm of his breathing, his sexy dark hair adorably mussed, his musky scent so wonderfully male. When she rolled a little towards him, thinking to trail her lips over the much-loved curve of his ear, he didn't move.

Strange.

Whenever she'd stayed at his place, the faintest noise or barest movement would wake him. She'd told him that burglars wouldn't stand a chance if they dared sneak around Devlin Stone's house in the dead of night. He thought nothing of his heightened primal instinct to be alert at the slightest provocation. His preparedness, even in a deep sleep, had made her feel so protected.

She smiled now at the irony of that thought as well as the warmth that washed through her watching him in this curiously vulnerable state. Was it that he'd had so little sleep or the fact that here in this isolated setting it was his turn to feel perfectly safe?

There wasn't a sign of movement other than his breathing and the hammer of her heartbeat in response to the urge to trace her tongue down the dent in his back, then curl her hand over his hip and wake him in a manner they'd both enjoy.

She tilted away.

To wake him at all would be selfish. He hadn't had enough sleep. *She* hadn't had enough sleep. Difference was her eyes were wide open, and the surf crashing on the shore seemed to call to her with a distant churning whisper.

One more day, one more day…

Carefully she slid out from beneath the sheet and slipped a sundress over her head. She brushed her hair and teeth and still Devlin lay on his side.

The waves called to her again and suddenly she wanted to know the feel of salty wind on her face, savour the heat of tropical sun on her skin. She wanted to capture as much of this place in her mind and with her senses as she possibly could. She never ever wanted to forget this amazing dream of living, even this short time, with Devlin in paradise.

She moved quietly out to the main room then down the steps, comparing the smell of burned-out torches to the romantic flickering of flames the night before. The most amazing night of her life.

Her one regret was her comment about 'some things being unwinnable'. As soon as the words had slipped out, she'd wanted to swallow them back down. She'd meant, of course, that she could never win Devlin's heart. Not fully. And she was close to certain that Devlin had known it.

But he hadn't reassured her. Hadn't confessed that, now they'd shared this unbelievable time together, he'd fallen hopelessly, irreversibly in love with her. Rather he'd considered her words before letting them slide.

Her fingertips brushed the dewy leaves as she wandered down the path to the beach, her bare toes digging into the powder-soft sand as her hair gently lifted on the sea breeze. Her stomach jumped when two small gecko lizards scuttled in front her, their skins reminding her of ghosts, their tails leaving faint trails in the sand.

When she reached the beach, a scattering of seagulls landed nearby. Their pink, or black, eyes studied her as they strutted around, so very comfortable in their world. A world where nothing mattered except—

'See any wild animals on your travels?'

Heart leaping to her throat, she spun around and let out a gasp. Devlin stood a few feet away, looking more delectable, illuminated in the sunrise, than any man had a right to.

She smiled. 'You're up.'

Rubbing the back of his neck as if working out a crick, he pretended to scowl. 'You didn't wake me.'

He looked larger than life and, for one more day, he was hers and no one else's.

When he looked at her oddly, she slanted her head and remembered to reply. 'You seemed sound asleep. We were up so late.'

'Or is that up early?'

He joined her, held her and kissed her until the seed of desire bloomed bright once more and she couldn't bear the thought of never feeling his skin on her skin again after tomorrow.

How could she say goodbye?

As if disgusted by their display of affection, a seagull squawked, swooping close. They broke apart, ducking as they laughed.

Devlin wrapped his arms around her, one brow lifted. 'Good thing we went to the lake yesterday or we might've been run out of town.'

When he rotated her in his arms so they both faced the surf, she held onto his hands, linked at her waist, glad he was awake and this wasn't a dream.

She rested her head back against his shoulder and gazed off at the peaceful horizon. 'It's hard to believe people on the mainland are waking up and getting ready to face the treadmill.'

His warm lips nipped her ear. 'Responsibilities do get in the way of a good time.'

'Guess you can't have fun all the time.'

She'd wanted to sound flippant, but her voice was thick and her nose stung with the sudden threat of tears. Which was *not* acceptable. She needed to immerse herself in this atmosphere, be grateful for the chance to finish this—finish *them* the way they deserved to end.

With no regrets.

Not this time.

His raspy chin snagged over the top of her head. 'Did Sabrina leave a message for you this morning?'

At a dig of unease, she worked away from his embrace and faced him. 'You mean on my cell phone? I didn't think we'd get reception way out here.'

'Even if we were out of range, R.J. is wealthy enough to have his own repeater station installed.'

'Did Nathan phone you?'

'He left a text message.'

'What did it say?'

She didn't mean for her voice to rise. She didn't want to think the worst.

Devlin rubbed the back of his neck again. 'I'm sure it's nothing.'

Her hands fisted at her sides. 'What did he say?'

He studied her tight lips and exhaled. 'He asked if you'd heard from Sabrina.'

Her bunched fingers unfurled as an awful feeling ribboned through her. She swallowed against the taste of bile rising in her throat and held her suddenly clammy forehead.

'Something's wrong.' She just knew it.

They'd had a fight. He'd made her cry. Maybe he wanted to know where she was to apologise. Or ask her to get her stuff out of his place.

'We don't know anything's wrong.' Devlin shrugged his broad shoulders. 'It could be good news.'

But it was clear from his furrowed expression that he hadn't convinced either of them.

She wove around him. 'I've got to call her.'

His hand snapped out and caught her wrist. 'When she's ready, she'll contact you.'

'Aren't you going to talk to Nathan?'

He seemed to think it through and dropped her hand. 'Let's see if she's left a message for you first.'

Exactly her thought. She sprinted off ahead of him.

'Hey!' he shouted. 'Wait for me.'

'Don't worry,' she called over her shoulder. 'I'm not afraid of wild animals, remember?'

The stab in her foot was swift, burning. Unable to stifle a yelp, she fell back onto her rump, holding her heel and biting her lip as searing pain shot an arrow up her leg.

Before she could figure out what had happened, Devlin dropped onto his knees beside her. All she knew was her foot hurt like blue blazes and her head was beginning to tingle at the pain.

While she sucked air in between her teeth, his hands went to the foot she cradled. 'What happened?'

Her adrenaline levels leapt as the knife in her foot sliced higher, reaching her knee.

'I'm not sure.' She swallowed water rising in her mouth. 'I-I think something bit me.'

He threw an urgent glance around. 'A snake?'

Carefully, he eased her hands and tourniquet grip away. A mini river of red was released, denting the soft white sand.

Cursing under his breath, he searched between long blades of grass and picked something up. The colour edging the offending item matched the changed colour of the sand.

His mouth pulled unhappily to one side. 'Looks like you were attacked by a shell.'

She rocked a little, hoping the motion would counter the

sharp edge of pain. 'Well, that's got to be better than stepping on a cobra.'

'No cobras around here. I'd thought possibly a brown snake.'

'Are they poisonous?'

He nodded. 'Deadly.'

While she hovered between the need to faint and the urge to run, he gently turned her foot to inspect the wound, then shook his head. 'That's a deep gash.'

'I'll live.' *Just.*

'Not if that gets infected. Septicaemia isn't pretty. We'll head for the mainland, find a doctor.'

Along with the pain, she cringed at a stab of guilt. She could barely meet his eyes.

'I'm sorry, Devlin.'

'Sorry for what?'

'I should've been more careful, watched where I was going.' Now he wanted to take her off the island. She'd ruined everything.

'It was an accident.'

'Guess I'm not much good at this adventure stuff, after all.'

'You're good at being you and that's good enough for me.' His gaze deepened before he blinked rapidly, then collected her in his arms. 'Just do me a favour and promise you won't take up base jumping or sailing around the Bermuda Triangle.'

She wrapped her arms around his neck, knowing that after tomorrow it wouldn't matter to him how she filled her time. She'd say goodbye, he'd make some noise, but ultimately he'd give up. Walk away. They'd done the drill before. It would be easier this time.

For him, anyway.

But for now…he was being so considerate and caring. She could placate him by telling him the truth.

'You don't have to worry. I promise to stay away from anything,' *and anyone,* 'that might cause me harm.'

When she saw relief flash in his eyes, she'd never felt closer to him…or farther away.

After Devlin carried her back to the bungalow and dressed the wound, using a well-equipped first-aid kit, Eden checked her cell phone. No message from Sabrina.

Her foot up on the sofa, her back against a downy pillow, she pressed the phone to her chin and debated aloud.

'I want to phone her.' Her finger itched to press fast-dial. 'But I'd rather she contact me again when she was ready.'

He brought over a glass of water. 'Good thinking.'

She stared at the phone, willing it to ring. 'I'm over-reacting, aren't I?'

'You love your sister. You worry for her.'

But he seemed distracted. A muscle popped repeatedly in his jaw and his eyes were darker than usual, the fathom-less blue full of shadows.

He handed over the water and nodded at her bandaged foot. 'That cut needs stitches.'

'It can wait—'

'No, it can't.' He crossed to the table and fished out a set of keys from the centrepiece bowl. 'We're taking the second boat and finding a doctor on the mainland.'

She set her jaw but then gave in. When he was in this frame of mind, nothing would dissuade him. She wouldn't argue. In fact, it was lovely to have him worry over her well-being like this. If she didn't know better, she might even begin to hope.

* * *

Noosa was the closest town. Devlin steered the six-metre motorboat away from the island's jetty and set off, eventually crossing the Noosa bar then travelling up the river until they moored at the town's north shore. He wouldn't hear of her putting any weight on her injured foot. Instead he lifted her in his arms and carried her in search of a doctor's office.

She wasn't quite certain if she was embarrassed or thrilled that their exhibition won more than a few gaping stares. One group of elderly ladies waiting at a bus stop actually applauded. But Devlin's focus didn't shift. He strode into the first doctor's surgery he found, quizzed the receptionist about the doctor's qualifications, then announced he had an emergency—a suspect snake bite.

Everyone leapt into action. The doctor saw her straight away. Her cheeks blazed when the doctor discovered not a snake bite but a nasty cut.

After the doctor called for his nurse, who cleaned and sutured the wound, she swung carefully out of the back rooms on crutches. Devlin flew to his feet, his ruggedly handsome face lined with concern. Which felt…nice. Strange. *Alice in Wonderland* upside down. Like yesterday at the lake. She was the one who was supposed to be worried about Devlin. Not the other way round.

'All good?' he asked, carefully taking her arm.

'Apparently.' She nodded at the counter. 'I need to—'

'The bill's been taken care of.' Angling his head, he inspected her crutches. 'I could carry you just as easily.'

'I'd have thought your arms would be falling off by now.'

His grin was wickedly confident. 'I was just limbering up.' He opened the door and she swung out ahead of him. 'We might as well have lunch here.'

She gave the tree-lined street a once-over. 'Noosa's renowned for its boutique shopping.'

'If you're up to it, we'll have a look around afterward.'

Any other time she'd have jumped at the chance. But today...

She smiled softly. 'I'd rather head back after lunch. Do you mind?'

His hand cupped her face as his dark eyes glittered with a smile. 'I don't mind in the least.'

CHAPTER ELEVEN

THEY had a leisurely lunch at one of Noosa's alfresco cafés and by the time they tied back up at the island, the better part of the day was lost. Devlin carried Eden to the bungalow, but only to collect the picnic blanket before carrying it, and her, to their lake.

They made themselves comfortable in a cool, fragrant patch of shade and made love, leisurely, milking out each and every moment. Afterwards they lay naked in each other's arms, speaking in hushed tones while Devlin peered up at the sky, one hand tucked behind his head while she rested her cheek on his chest, drawing aimless circles through the wiry dark hair.

Later, he walked with her into the water, holding her in his arms while she held her bandaged foot high. When they were three parts submerged, he kissed her and twirled her around, the rush of the waterfall and cricket song the perfect accompaniments to her burst of laughter before, smiling, he kissed her again.

They ate back at the bungalow, watching the torch flames flicker until the shadows consumed the light and he carried her to bed. Devlin kissed her tenderly, held her close to his hard, hot body and a beautiful sense of belonging settled over her.

Next Eden knew, it was morning. She'd woken to the sound of a boat approaching.

Her chest tightened painfully and a rush of tears flooded her eyes. She couldn't remember falling asleep. How could she have nodded off so easily and wasted what precious time they'd had left? She could sleep all day tomorrow, but the hours they'd lost last night she would never have again.

But when, wrapped in his strong arms, she looked up and saw he was awake and smiling down at her, a little of her upset faded. She didn't want to hold onto any bad feelings these last few moments. She wanted to cling onto the wonder—cling onto Devlin—for as long and as hard as she could.

His voice was thick and gravelled. 'Morning.'

She swallowed against the lump in her throat and told her mouth not to quiver when she smiled. 'Morning.'

'Gregory and Tianne are back.'

She burrowed into the comforting plateau of his chest, clamping shut her eyes, wishing desperately this morning belonged to yesterday.

'I heard,' she murmured.

His knuckle found her chin and he lifted her face until she had no choice but to look into his eyes.

His sombre gaze penetrated hers. 'We need to talk.'

Her pounding heart leapt to her throat. She ached to hear what he had to say and at the same time wanted to block her ears. It wouldn't be what she longed to hear. Nothing to do with 'love' and 'for ever'. Far more likely it'd be a 'thank you, this has been nice'. She was only torturing herself to even think the other way.

Her stomach twisted and she dropped her gaze from his. 'Shouldn't we get dressed, pack?'

'I don't want this to end,' he said simply, and her heart fluttered madly as her gaze shot back to his. 'I want to see you again, Eden.'

'You do?' she squeaked, and he nodded.

But she didn't see happiness sparking in his gaze. She wasn't sure what emotion brewed in the depths of his eyes, but, whatever it was, it made her skin goose-bump in an uncomfortable way, as if for some reason she needed to defend herself, or remind him of why she'd buckled and had come away with him. It hadn't been to trap him.

'You know what I said our first night here,' she reminded him.

'You needed to see what we started in that hotel suite through to its natural conclusion. But it's gone beyond that.'

Her throat closed and, despite everything in her system warning caution, a tiny hopeful smile lifted the corners of her mouth. 'You're really serious.'

He rolled onto his side to face her, up on an elbow, his head resting in his palm. 'You also said you wanted to let go. Have fun. We *have* had fun, haven't we, Eden?'

She couldn't deny it. She shrugged one shoulder. 'The best time of my life.'

A muscle in his jaw pulsed as his gaze intensified. 'But you said you didn't want anything…lasting.'

Eden blinked. Well, yes, she had said that. But that was before they'd reconnected in this incredible way—a way that surpassed by leaps and bounds their previous relationship. But perhaps he was about to point that out too, so she wouldn't interrupt. Instead she merely nodded.

'And yet saying goodbye now seems like an impossibility,' he reasoned, then studied her still harder. 'Doesn't it?'

Her sigh was a silent blissful release. They *were* on the same track.

'Yes,' she said, barely able to believe this was happening. 'I agree.'

His lidded gaze roamed her face as he curled hair behind her ear, as if the action might help him over this last important step. 'I've done some soul-searching, going over our past relationship in my mind, where we went wrong. We're different people now.'

Building emotion blocked off her air in the most wonderful way. Dying to hear his next words, feeling the tingle of sheer happiness filling her like much-needed rain filling a well, she nodded again.

'Then we'll take this to the next level. The level I know now we're both comfortable with.' A frown pinched his brow. 'I'm not misreading you, am I?'

Her heart was hammering, sending an overload of heat to her cheeks and her neck. She hiccupped out a laugh. 'Guess it's pretty hard to miss.'

Yes, she wanted to take this to the next level. She wanted them to get back together. As he'd said, he wasn't the same person. He'd matured. She'd never forget the way he'd cared for her after her accident. At last he must appreciate a little of the worry she'd endured three years ago.

But what they'd shared here felt better than right. It felt fated. The words she'd longed to hear must come next.

I love you, Eden. I love you with all my heart.

Lord above, she loved him too. Trying to hold back the tide had been useless, particularly when Devlin couldn't deny it any longer either.

His head tipped closer and he kissed her gently. That one simple caress—the barest touching of lips—promised her the world.

He drew away and smiled into her eyes. 'Then it's settled. We'll continue letting go—having fun—when we return to Sydney.'

Eden's surroundings seemed to lock in freeze-frame. Even the relentless roar of crashing waves seemed to stop. *Let's continue to have fun* hadn't been what she'd expected to hear.

'You're a special woman,' Devlin went on. 'We were at odds when we broke up three years ago but now we seem to connect close to the middle. And, given we want the same thing, there's no reason we can't enjoy ourselves for however long it lasts.'

When she grew dizzy, she began to breathe again. He wanted to continue this affair. Wanted to continue the good times. But that was all? That was *it*? And how could she hate him or argue with his train of thought when he'd merely followed hers to this apparently logical conclusion?

She *had* wanted to let go. Have fun. She'd vowed she wasn't after anything serious. And the crazy, difficult, tempting part was…

If she couldn't have his love, if she couldn't have the wedding vows, would having his sexy smile and companionship be better than nothing? That was what Sabrina was enjoying now with Nate. Her sister was happy to go with the flow and make the most of what she had while she had it.

He lightly squeezed her shoulder. 'You're unsure?'

A part of her wanted to reassure him, but the words stuck in her throat. She did want to see him again. He'd opened up the possibility and if she said goodbye, this time the door would close for ever. God help her, could she bear to live with that?

His hand slid a sensual path down her arm. 'I'll go tell Greg and Tianne to come back in a couple of days to give you more time to decide.'

What he meant was give him more time to persuade her, to make love to her and strip her of any final shreds of opposition.

Torn, she looked around and, weird, but the room had taken on a slightly different aura, as if the tall wooden birds were disapproving of the possibility of her surrender. She'd thought herself so strong. In many ways she was, but where Devlin was concerned she could be an emotional weakling. Still, as agonising as it was, as much as she wished it were different, the reality was clear.

They couldn't hold onto what they'd found here. Their time, as sweet as it had been, was over. She needed to leave with her memories.

Leave and save what was left of her heart.

She forced her rubbery lips to move. 'I'm sorry, Devlin, I really am,' she croaked over a suddenly dry throat. 'But we've been here before.'

Three years ago, to be precise, when he'd choked at any hint of lasting commitment. Nothing had changed.

He blinked several times and then smiled a crooked smile meant to melt. 'I'll go and tell Greg he needs to come back on Thursday, or Friday—'

She set a palm against his chest and almost regretted it. He felt strong and hard and right. So very tempting.

Shoring up her strength, she withdrew her hand. 'We both needed this—to have this final time together—but I can't pretend. I don't want to be anyone's permanent good-time girl. Who I am—my heart—hasn't changed. I want to settle down and find my happily-ever-after. One day I want a family of my own.'

His brows fell together. 'I don't understand. I thought we were agreed. After these last couple of days and seeing how happy your sister is with Nate, happy to just enjoy their time together—'

She was shaking her head. 'Truth is I'm not Sabrina. Nate isn't you. They might be happy to see how things pan out between them, but your offer just now proves to me like nothing else could that I need more. If I accepted—' She swallowed against the suffocating rising ache. 'If I continued to see you,' she went on, 'I'd only end up hurt again and it wouldn't be your fault. It'd be mine for not being stronger.'

His gaze changed and the dark blue of his eyes turned almost cold. 'You want marriage.'

At his tone, pride rose up, goading her to quit sounding like some manipulative desperate spinster. She was an intelligent woman with great prospects and good friends and family. She didn't need a man to make her whole.

But she *did* want what most people wanted. To share her life with a special someone. She wanted children and walks with a stroller to the park. She wanted anniversaries and to grow old with someone who would never turn his back on her. Who would defend and love her until they said their final goodnight.

As tears banked up, closing her throat, her mouth quivered into a wistful smile. 'Yes, Devlin. I want marriage.' *I want the dream.*

His nostrils flared. She pictured his mind thrashing over her confession as he pushed up higher on his elbow.

'I can't do that.'

'I know.' Hell, she'd always known. 'I'm not angry.' *Please don't be angry with me.* 'For these last couple of days we *did* find common ground. Now it's time to let go.'

'Nothing will change your mind?'

Nothing except a sincere admission that marriage was at least a possibility in their future. But that wasn't going to happen.

She shook her head slowly. 'I'm afraid not.'

His eyes challenged hers, testing her resolve. Then something shifted in their beautiful blue depths…as if he'd lost the battle and was prepared to lay his heart on the line too. He came a little closer and his head angled as his eyes swept over her face.

Her fingers itched to touch his bristled cheek, graze the soft bow of his kissable mouth. Perhaps if she said the words first, told him she'd loved him for such a long time— could never love anyone else—then he'd *have* to see what they had together was more than fun. It was real. And it could be lasting. He only needed the courage to accept it. Accept that committing himself to another didn't need to mean entrapment and hurt as it had for his parents.

She and Devlin could be happy.

But then he inhaled sharply, tugged his ear and came up with a casual smile. 'Well…hell, what can I say?'

She swallowed back tears. She could think of at least three words.

'I respect your decision,' he said, finding her hand. Gaze lowered on the action, he kissed each knuckle, holding the last against his lips for a long torturous moment before he murmured, 'Can't say it wasn't nice while it lasted.'

Then, without meeting her gaze, he flung back the sheet and sauntered to the bathroom while Eden bit her lip and closed her eyes, detesting that she couldn't stop the tears from falling on her pillow.

Couldn't stop her heart from breaking all over again.

CHAPTER TWELVE

EDEN tried to make the rest of their time together light, even while Devlin's mood remained flat. But that wasn't quite right. He seemed detached, shut down. He was still polite, but his eyes whenever they met hers were blank, as if he refused to see her—refused to acknowledge her feelings—and that hurt more than anything.

Had she been wrong to come here? Were the memories worth the pain of losing him all over again?

Eden wondered what Tianne and Gregory thought of Devlin's remote air when they asked about their time on the island. Gregory was the consummate professional, letting nothing negative bleed through to his expression. Tianne, on the other hand, couldn't contain the concern from showing in her deep brown eyes.

Once in the air and on their way back to Sydney after refuelling in Noosa, Eden felt too disheartened to be scared and too preoccupied to appreciate the scenery drifting below. The time seemed to both drag out and crunch into a compact finite state that ended when his Lexus pulled up outside her apartment block.

As the engine idled she looked straight ahead as did he, her heartbeat ticking by the seconds.

'Thank you,' she murmured.

His tanned hands twisted on the wheel. 'You're welcome.' He added, 'Look after yourself.'

'I will. You too.'

He reached for his door handle. 'I'll see you to the building door.'

But her hand caught his hard thigh and she felt his steely limb stiffen beneath her touch.

'Please,' she said, dragging her hand away. 'Don't.'

His jaw clenched, but he closed the door and nodded. 'As you wish.'

Eden did a double take. This wasn't the Devlin she knew. This man didn't even sound like Devlin. But this was all there was. He was making it crystal clear. His no meant no.

She took air into her lungs, opened her door, hooked her overnight bag over her arm and hobbled on her heel through the gate towards her building.

Her heart wrenched when his car's engine roared away.

Sensing some movement above her head, she lifted her heavy gaze to a nearby tree branch. A sparrow looked down at her, as still as still, his pretty black eyes glittering as if he could feel her pain and wished he could help. But nothing would help. Nothing but time.

And now she had so much of it.

Eden saw the note on the table as soon as she entered her apartment five minutes later. Sabrina had left it along with her keys and some cash. She wanted to contribute to this coming utility bill and wrote that she'd almost called Eden about it but knew she would've only told her to keep the money.

Mystery surrounding Nate's text message to Devlin solved. Nothing bad, only Sabrina being considerate, as usual.

Sabrina also wrote that she had two assignments due that week, so it was head down and she'd call soon.

Eden folded the note and, although devoid of energy, she grabbed the house extension and punched in Temptations' number.

Tracey squealed down the line. 'You're back! How was the dirty weekend away? I want to hear all about it.'

'It was fabulous.' Eden hoped she sounded convincing. She didn't want to get into a heart-to-heart with Tracey now. She only wanted to curl up into a ball on her bed and stay there until this time next week.

'I hurt my foot though,' Eden added, setting up her excuse.

'Oh, no! Are you all right?'

'I'm going to take the rest of the week off to let it rest.'

'Well, sure. No problem. Everything's under control here.'

Tears she'd kept at bay all day crowded the back of her throat, as if her body knew it was almost time to lower its defences and let all that pent-up emotion out.

'Eden,' Tracey murmured, 'are you okay?'

'Perfectly wonderful,' she cried, with as much false enthusiasm as she could muster. 'But I do need to pop a pain-killer. My foot's beginning to throb.'

After goodbyes, she hung up and set her mind to a final task. She limped to her desk, drew out her diary and began to write.

Dear Diary,

I've done it again. I'm in love with Devlin up to my silly little neck. In the back of my mind I always knew this would happen. Maybe that's why I contacted him. Not to ask him to warn Nate away from Sabrina, but to see him again without losing face. I could've said no anywhere along the way, but my heart kept saying yes.

If I wasn't so certain that we'd both regret his suggestion to continue the affair, I might have relented. But the simple truth is that I need more, and he's nowhere near ready for a gold band. But I still believe in him...that one day he will be ready to settle. Just wish it could be with me ☹

CHAPTER THIRTEEN

THAT Thursday morning, ten past eleven, Eden hadn't eaten breakfast, was onto her fourth cup of coffee and didn't think she'd get changed out of her PJs again today.

What was the point? She wasn't seeing anyone. There'd be time enough next week to scrub up. She would brush her hair, dig out the lip gloss, when she went back to work.

If she went back to work next week.

She couldn't seem to rouse enthusiasm for anything. Except weepie movies. That particular form of sensory overload was her way, she'd decided, of weening herself off Devlin. And she *would* succeed.

He hadn't called once. In fact, this morning's Yahoo items included a photograph of Devlin in a dinner jacket escorting a buxom redhead to an opening at the Opera House. She'd held back the tears for an hour before they'd sneaked up and surprised her when she was folding the laundry—a far cry from her life of leisure in paradise. Despite his fancy words that last morning, how much had that time meant to Devlin? Had he taken that redhead home to his bed last night?

She was pouring a glass of orange juice when the intercom sounded. Her heart leapt, juice splashed over the counter and her mind jumped to conclusions. But, of course it wasn't Devlin. Clearly he had put her, and their experience, behind him. He'd moved on.

How she envied him that.

Eden shuffled to the intercom by the door and depressed the speaker key. 'Who is it?'

'Sabrina.'

Eden slumped. They'd spoken briefly on the phone since she'd arrived home, but Sabrina had had those assignments to finish and so hadn't come to visit. Good thing, Eden thought, casting an eye around the dirty dishes on the coffee table, the magazines strewn over the floor near the couch. The place was a sty. She was usually such a tidy bug. If Sabrina saw this mess she'd know something was up.

She didn't feel like sharing yet, particularly not when Sabrina was obviously so happy with Nate. She didn't want to prick her sister's balloon.

She chewed her lip, searching for an excuse. 'Sabrina, I'm, uh, not feeling so well—'

'Sorry. Not listening,' Sabrina cut in. 'You didn't sound like yourself on the phone. You were tight-lipped about your time away with Devlin. You've taken time off work. Now you're opening up and letting me in.'

Eden raised her brows. 'I thought as the older sister it was my place to boss *you* around.'

'From this point on consider it a shared responsibility.'

Giving in to a grin, Eden hit a button and let Sabrina into the building. A moment later, Sabrina stood at the door, her expression pained. 'Eden, you look awful.'

'Nice to see you too.'

Sabrina took her hand in both of hers. 'Oh, Ee, what's happened?'

Eden pushed out a sigh. 'You mean everything or only the really bad part?'

As they moved towards the couch Sabrina held her up. 'What's wrong with your foot?'

'I'll get to that.'

After heaping magazines out of the way, they sat side by side. Eden started with how she'd phoned Devlin last week, wanting him to talk to Nate about letting Sabrina off the hook.

Sabrina paled. 'I can't believe you'd do that.'

'Looking back, neither can I. I'm sorry. I only wanted to protect you.'

'You can't protect me from every bruise.'

'That's what Devlin said.'

Sabrina seemed to think it through, then nodded. 'What did he say about the two of you? I take it the weekend didn't go well.'

'The weekend went brilliantly! I felt as if I were living a dream. He was charming, of course, and sexy and making love was like—' She let her shoulders drop and lowered her eyes. 'You don't need to hear that.'

'You're in love with him,' Sabrina said simply.

Eden gave in to the truth. 'You were right. I don't think I ever stopped loving him. I tried to block it out, beat it down, cage it in.'

'And now it's out there.' Sabrina lowered her voice. 'Does Devlin know?'

'God, no! That's the one thing saving me. After he thought I was bitten by that snake—'

'You were bitten by a *what*?'

'Turned out I'd stood on a broken shell.'

Holding her heart, Sabrina gazed down at her sister's

bandaged foot and understood. 'Better than a set of fangs, I suppose.'

'There was quite a bit of blood. Devlin was worried. Didn't help that I'd been jumping off cliffs.'

Sabrina wailed, 'Were you out of your *mind*?'

'A little. And I've never been happier. That's why I can't regret it.'

'Regret agreeing to go away with him?'

She nodded. 'And I can't regret telling Devlin that we can't see each other again. He didn't want to say goodbye. He wanted to keep his bedroom door wide open…but with no strings attached.'

'He's still not interested in commitment,' Sabrina surmised, 'and you still are.'

Eden turned more towards her sister. 'Has Nate told you about their father?'

'He said neither he nor Devlin really knew their dad. He's aloof. Cold, really.'

'Devlin told me he never wants to make the same mistake his father made.'

'Get married?'

She expanded. 'Before he's ready. If, in fact, a man like his father would ever have been ready. He sounds like a real creep.' At least Devlin wasn't horrible; he was merely a delectable bachelor, through and through.

Sabrina was shaking her head. 'Maybe I'm just a hopeless romantic, but why don't you just see each other and worry about talk of marriage later? Nate and I aren't close to that yet.'

'You and Nate don't have a history.' Eden lifted her chin. 'Believe me, it's best we both remember those days away for what they were—a delayed goodbye.'

'But maybe if he knew that you love him—'

'It's over!' Eden flinched at her raised voice and set a finger to her throbbing temple. 'I'm sorry, hon. I'm rotten company today.'

Sabrina pushed to her feet. 'You go rest. I'll ring tomorrow to see how you are.'

Eden stood too and, holding her sister's hand, kissed Sabrina's cheek. 'Thanks for being the best sister a girl could wish for.'

Sabrina didn't look convinced. 'Only you're forgetting that if I hadn't started dating Nate you wouldn't have seen Devlin again and be going through this heartache, take two.'

She gripped Sabrina's hand harder. 'This has nothing to do with you. You enjoy what you have with Nate. One day I'll find the right one.'

But as she saw Sabrina to the door Eden knew in her heart she *had* found the right one. She just hadn't been right for him.

Devlin stood on the seventh-floor balcony of one of Monte Carlo's most exclusive hotels, along with other special guests, watching this year's Formula One cars scream around the city, navigating the hairpins, passing the luxurious multimillion-dollar yachts moored in the harbour.

Relishing the near-deafening roar of the engines, Devlin counted his blessings. His pit-crew friend was a real mate, extending him an offer to hobnob with his racing team's VIPs during the French Riviera's most revered social and sporting event.

The annual race was held on the narrow course laid out on the winding streets of Monaco, and, although the average speeds were relatively low, the *Grand Prix de*

Monaco was the jewel of the Formula One crown, as well as possibly the most dangerous of the circuit.

The history, the spectacle, the over-the-top competition…what man worth his metal wouldn't enjoy such a time? He might not be behind a wheel, challenging every fibre of his mind and body to perform their best, but surely this was the next best thing.

But as he sipped his French beer and gazed at the cars flying down the start-finish straight his mind drifted to memories of a quieter place.

A paradise on earth.

But the feelings that place created weren't sustainable. Eden had known that. If she were any less of a woman, she'd have accepted his suggestion that they continue to see each other on their return. If she wasn't so smart she'd have believed they could hold onto the magic. Perhaps even work her way closer to a proposal of marriage.

As soon as she'd fessed up—that she wanted *for ever* or nothing at all—he'd taken the only reasonable course of action. He'd stepped aside. Completely.

No use prolonging the pain. Not that he'd lain awake worrying afterwards. Not like last time. He'd got stuck back into life over the last few weeks. He'd hit the social scene, taking an associate's visiting sister to an opening at the Opera House. He played squash four nights a week, and if that failed to fell him he worked into the night.

There was no use dwelling on it. He wouldn't—he *couldn't*—do the 'love stroke commitment' thing. He wouldn't make his father's mistake and misinterpret intense physical attraction for something more, then bring children into what could ultimately turn out to be an emotionally barren home. Hell, if he couldn't give his heart to a woman like Eden—if he wasn't prepared to take the risk with her—then the truth was clear.

He was incapable of committing to romantic love.

End of chapter.

Turn the page.

Devlin wandered to the railing, rested his forearms on the carved stone balustrade. He absently gazed into his beer as the smell of fumes slipped past on the breeze before the sound of screeching tyres seized his attention.

Below, a car was spinning wildly, circles of tyre smoke rising off the bitumen as a captive audience gasped. When the car slammed into the barrier, the crash seemed to shake the windows. Everyone on the balcony murmured or held their breath, waiting for the car to burst into flame or the driver to leap out.

An audible sigh went up when the driver scrambled from the wreck, sprinting away before removing his helmet and dashing it to the ground. The men on the balcony held their heads and moaned. What a terrible tragedy. The lead car was out of the race.

An attractive woman in a red satin dress joined in the speculation. Her olive skin was smooth, her ebony hair a shimmering dark river down her back. A weighty diamond necklace circled her throat. As if sensing his gaze, the woman looked over and smiled. The suggestion in her slumberous green eyes was clear.

Are you free?

Devlin held her gaze.

Yes, damn it. Freer than I've ever been.

He set his glass down and crossed over, then tipped his chin at the scene below. 'It's unfortunate.'

She seemed more interested in him than the race. 'Are you English?' Her own English was perfect but laced with a sultry southern French accent.

'I'm Australian. From Sydney.'

One sleek eyebrow arched as she rested her champagne flute against her chin. 'I like Australians.'

A photographer interrupted and rattled off something that translated into wanting to take their picture. Devlin bristled as he did whenever a lens was shoved under his nose, but when the lady consented he relented. He looped an arm around her waist, she leant in and the camera flashed.

As the photographer moved on the woman remained close. 'This week is so much fun,' she purred. 'Are you attending the ball?'

'Wouldn't miss it for the world.'

Her fingers, holding the flute, brushed his arm. 'Perhaps we can share a dance?'

Terrific idea.

So why did his smile feel like a mask on his face? There wasn't a reason in the world he shouldn't dance with this woman. Any number of men might challenge him for the privilege. And yet he felt…odd. Strange, as he'd never felt before. As if he were cheating, and that wasn't possible, not when he wasn't dating anyone. When he wasn't anywhere near committed.

He broke through the malaise and found a slanted smile. 'I could collect you from your hotel.'

'If you escort me there this afternoon,' she offered, 'you'll know where to come.'

His heart began to pound. He wanted to say the words, make it clear, tell the world.

'Just so you know,' he said, 'I'm not the marrying kind.'

She looked confused, then laughed softly and leaned in extra close. 'Oh, *mon ami*, what man is?'

CHAPTER FOURTEEN

'EE, HAVE you ever been late?'

Eden looked across the café table at her sister. 'I like to be on time.' She smiled. 'You know that.'

Not once had they missed the school bus. Library books were always returned on time. As she'd got older, she'd remained almost painfully punctual. Being organised and focused had helped this last month.

After ending it with Devlin, Eden's spirits were still low, but she was back on track, doing what needed to be done. She'd put in an order for some exciting spring fashion, and had even made final arrangements to fly to LA next month to check on a few leading fashion houses. She wanted to do Rodeo Drive.

Stirring her vanilla Chi, Sabrina qualified her question. 'I mean late with your period.'

Eden scooped more chocolate mud cake onto her fork. 'Oh, sure. My cycle's never been regular.' Then the reason behind Sabrina's question hit like a hammer blow. Eden dropped her dessert fork on its plate with a clatter.

Even while her stomach sank to her knees, Eden tried not to sound panicked. 'Sabrina, honey, are *you* late?'

'I was. I even bought a home pregnancy test. Turned out I didn't need it. False alarm.'

Blessed relief flooded Eden's system and the tension pinning back her shoulders relaxed before she forked up more mud cake. 'Did Nathan know?'

Ten weeks into their relationship the fires of love still burned bright. Eden was happy for Sabrina. Happy for them both. She'd seen them together a few times and had to admit they made a gorgeous couple. That day in the hotel suite Nathan had said he cared for her sister. Now Eden believed him.

Seemed she'd been wrong to crucify him over those tabloid stories. Recently, with Nathan retired from the limelight, the paparazzi had hooked onto the older Stone brother to get their dose of gossip. Eden had wanted to hurl that magazine in the trash when a photo of Devlin with that sleazy-looking French woman had appeared in the society pages. His smile, as well as the woman's exposed cleavage, told Eden all she needed to know.

She stabbed her glazed cherry now while Sabrina shook her head. 'I didn't tell Nate about my pregnancy suspicions. I did some research first and found out that a woman's breasts get tender and swell. Goes with an increase in appetite, then steady weight gain.'

About to slide cake into her opened mouth, Eden's fork paused and her head cocked. 'Tender breasts, you say?'

Eden glanced down at her snug-fitting bodice, which, come to think of it, hadn't been so snug last time she'd worn this outfit.

'Not everyone gets morning sickness,' Sabrina went on. 'But some women get it in the evenings, some the whole day through. And then there's the cravings. Ice cream and sweets are popular.'

Eden's horrified gaze swung to her cake as blood rushed to her cheeks. She'd still felt famished after her baked pumpkin risotto. She'd wanted something sweet, and lots of it.

As a wave of pins and needles took over her limbs, the café's surroundings seemed to close in. 'You said you didn't use that pregnancy test?' she croaked, remembering that one time she and Devlin hadn't used protection.

'Still have it, right here in my bag.' Sabrina's eyes narrowed as she studied her sister's pallor. 'Ee, aren't you well?'

Eden grabbed for her napkin and held it to her mouth as chocolate cake churned in her stomach. She knew her eyes had gone wide.

'Maybe nothing,' she mumbled into the linen.

Sabrina's furrowed brow morphed into a full-blown gape. 'Oh, my…don't tell me. *You're* late?'

Eden's stomach roiled and she groaned. 'I didn't think anything of it.' *Until this minute.*

'And your breasts?'

'Touchy—' she glanced down again '—and bigger.'

With a determined face, Sabrina reached for her handbag. 'Will we use the bathroom here or can you wait till we get home to do the test?'

A fierce emotion seized Eden's heart at the same time her palms began to sweat. It was the same feeling she had as a child when the roller-coaster climbed that first steep scary hill before it dropped.

She held her dipping tummy and bit her lip. 'Sabrina… I'm frightened.'

Sabrina's firm expression softened. 'No need to be. I'm here for you, Ee. Devlin will be too.'

Clamping shut her eyes, she cringed. She and Devlin parents? Devlin the father of her baby...a baby who would be born out of wedlock. This wasn't the way it was supposed to be. Yes, she'd daydreamed of having his child—but only after they were married and Devlin was a proud father and, oh, God, this was all wrong!

Grabbing her water, Eden set the cold glass to her clammy forehead. 'Please, let's not bring him into this until...'

'Until you're sure?'

Eden nodded, fighting the nausea rising to her throat. She wished Sabrina hadn't mentioned morning sickness.

Next Eden knew, Sabrina was by her side, helping her to her feet. 'Nothing's certain yet. Could be a false alarm, like mine.'

But as they moved to the desk to square the bill Eden knew Sabrina didn't believe it. She *was* with child. Devlin Stone's child. She knew it as surely as she knew her own name. Just as she knew Devlin would *not* be pleased.

Out on the busy Sydney footpath, Eden clutched her sister's hand. 'Promise me you won't try to contact Devlin about this.'

Sabrina's eyes flooded with compassion. 'He needs to know.'

'And I need time to sort this out. Figure out what to do next.'

Sabrina exhaled and slowly nodded. 'I promise, but on one condition. If you are having a baby, I want to be godmother.'

Eden wanted to laugh and cry at the same time. How she loved her little sister.

'The godmother title comes with a lot of diaper changing and burping duty,' she warned.

Sabrina curled her arm through Eden's and walked her to the car. 'What are sisters for?'

CHAPTER FIFTEEN

'ARE you asleep?'

Eden sighed at the deep voice in her dream. It belonged to Devlin and he was standing over her while she lay by their lake on *le Paradis sur Terre*. He was smiling down, his strong bronzed arms reaching out.

'Eden?' The dream's voice came again.

'Yes, Devlin,' she murmured as the palm fronds rustled overhead and the blue sky shone even brighter. But she heard voices in the background and there shouldn't be anyone else on the island. They were supposed to be alone, and time was running out...

She groaned, feeling both light as air and heavy as a brick when Devlin scooped her up off the soft blanket and into his capable arms. He didn't speak again, merely gazed down at her, dark eyes twinkling. She knew what was in store. He planned to take her back to the bungalow where they would make love again and again.

On a delicious sigh, she twisted more into his hard bare chest, soaking up his masculine scent, wishing this time would never end. Then she remembered and frowned.

'They' had already ended. There was another challenge

facing her now. She was having a baby, *Devlin's* baby, and she needed to tell him…tell him soon.

But how…when?

The rocking motion bumped her cheek against his chest and the woodsy scent became somehow stronger, more real. A moment ago vibrant scarlet blooms had twined between lush thick foliage. Now everything seemed dark.

Shuddering, she clamped shut her eyes as her stomach twinged and her heart began to thump.

She should open her eyes, face what was ahead, but she felt so very tired…

Another bump and her heavy eyelids dragged open. Her cheek rested against something dark and smooth. She was indeed being carried, but she wasn't on their island. There were high ceilings, mahogany furniture and, in a large space, a desk with people standing around, some peering over—

Her gaze sprang up and she gasped.

'Devlin!'

His long stride didn't falter. 'So, Sleeping Beauty's awake.'

Shoving the remnants of grogginess away, she pushed against his chest, which wasn't bare as it had been in her dream. He wore a shirt and jacket and, oh, Lord, she remembered now!

'What are *you* doing here?' she cried, pushing harder, which proved to be as big a deterrent as her previous effort. Was it this man's mission in life to sweep her up into his arms whenever and wherever he pleased?

'At the moment,' he replied, his gait determined, 'I'm finding you some fresh air. You're obviously unwell.'

Snoozing in public, probably moaning in her sleep… guess it might have looked that way.

Mortally tired by five-thirty that afternoon, she'd only

wanted to go home and collapse. But a friend had invited her to his exhibition and she hadn't wanted to let Zack down. They'd known each other since college and tonight was his debut into the art world.

So, dragging herself home from Temptations, she'd pulled on her lilac Lisa Ho cross-over cocktail dress—more room around the middle—and had cabbed it to this inner-city hotel. Two ice waters and what should have been lively conversation with other guests hadn't curbed her desire to curl up. She hadn't been able to keep from yawning. So she'd had the concierge call a cab and had indeed curled up on a comfy foyer settee. Little wonder she'd nodded off.

'I'm fine,' she told Devlin now, trying desperately to ignore the glorious heat radiating from beneath his shirt. 'You can let me down. I'm just…tired.'

Grunting, he strode through automatic glass doors that led to an unoccupied courtyard. The fresh air immediately filled her lungs and, damn it, she did feel a smidgen better.

Unfortunately she could do little about the physical effects of her pregnancy…the appetite, the nausea, the chronic fatigue, which this week had been merciless. At the boutique, she took naps in the back room, telling Tracey that a bug was responsible for her lack of energy. From the worried slant of Tracey's brows, she knew her assistant wasn't convinced.

When the time was right Eden would tell her friend. She needed to tell the father of her baby the good news first, but she wasn't ready for that confrontation yet.

When the home test had proved positive, she'd had her GP confirm the result. But she'd suffered some bleeding this last week, the twelfth gestational week, and a scan had been scheduled in a couple of days to give her the all-clear. When she saw her baby—knew that he or she was truly safe—then, and only then, would she let Devlin know he would soon be a father. What bad luck that she and Devlin should happen to be at the same hotel on the same night.

Unless…

'You didn't answer my question,' she said as he stopped before a bench and set her carefully down to sit. 'What are you doing here?'

'Meeting a friend for dinner in the ground-floor restaurant. You?'

'Art exhibition,' she replied, thinking he sounded sincere. That he hadn't followed her and mustn't know anything about her secret. But then why would he? She and Sabrina were the only ones who knew he was the father and Sabrina would never betray her trust. She'd promised not to tell.

Lowering down beside her, he quizzed her eyes. 'This exhibition must be important to drag yourself out when you're at death's door.'

'Zack Perry, the artist, is a good friend.'

He cocked a curious brow. 'I see.'

'And I'm not on death's door. I'm simply—'

'I know, I know. You're tired.' But he looked as convinced by her excuse as Tracey had been this past week. 'Would you like some water?'

'I would *like* to go home.'

She went to stand but his hand on her shoulder eased her back down.

'Sit for a while before you go rushing off.'

'I'm not sick,' she insisted. Not in the way he thought.

He slid a sizzling glance down her dress and legs then back up. Damn the man, she was instantly on fire.

One dark eyebrow lifted. 'I must say, you don't look as though you're fading away.'

She tucked her chin in. Was her weight gain that obvious? Devlin, on the other hand, looked in prime condition—mouth-watering in pressed dark trousers, a casual custom-made jacket and open-necked shirt. He looked so good, smelled so fine, heaven help her, she had to fight the urge to snuggle back into those wholly masculine arms.

'How's your foot?'

His question broke her trance and she cleared her throat.

'Better, thanks.' And, now he was here, she had to ask. 'I see you were in Monaco.'

His eyes narrowed on hers.

Yes, that's right, her eyes said back. *I saw the photograph of you with your arm around Miss Mammary of Monte Carlo.* From his perceptive grin he'd also guessed the photo had turned her green.

'I dropped in for a couple of days,' he explained.

Her own smile was tight. 'Those short stints seem to suit you.'

His mouth hooked up higher, then, angling more towards her, he rested his arm along the back of the bench. 'Have you done any globe-trotting recently?'

'I postponed a trip to LA,' she admitted.

Not only did the thought of jet lag make her shudder, no matter how much her doctor assured her, she wouldn't fly while she was pregnant. She wondered what Devlin's opinion on the subject would be.

But he didn't appear to have anything remotely cautious on his mind. His gaze was roaming her face as if he were remembering the feel of her skin, the way she'd arched longingly beneath him and quivered whenever his warm, giving mouth had trailed down her neck.

'Did you book in for those climbing lessons?' he asked as his deliberate gaze skimmed her jaw.

She inhaled, determined to contain her dangerous thoughts, even if he wasn't. 'I've put them on hold too.'

Permanent hold. She was responsible for another life. She had to look after herself so she could look after her baby. Would Devlin change any aspect of his lifestyle when he found out that he was going to be a dad? Would he feel the mantle of responsibility as intensely as she did?

An image flashed to mind—Devlin stuck in the millennium's worst blizzard atop some distant godforsaken mountain.

Squirming, she curled some hair behind her ear.

What if he wanted to tone down his adventures for the sake of his unborn child? Didn't he deserve the opportunity to make that kind of decision earlier rather than later? Maybe she should find the courage to tell him now before the scan.

Maybe he would thank her.

Willing her heartbeat to slow, she dropped her gaze. She didn't want to see his reaction if it wasn't good.

'Devlin, I need to tell you—'

'Don't worry.' His arm slid away from the bench's back railing.

Her gaze lifted to study his implacable expression. 'Don't worry about what?'

'I'm not keeping you out here to take advantage of the situation.'

Her brows lifted. Devlin had climbed back on the dating pony mere days after they'd said goodbye again. On the island, he'd taken his best shot, hoping to keep her in his bed. But clearly he wouldn't be gutted if he never saw her again.

No matter how much her heart begged her to offer him her lips and claim the kiss she'd been dreaming of, it would mean little to him other than a means to an end. A way to extend the affair. As she'd made it clear before, she couldn't bring herself to be anyone's mistress. Not even Devlin Stone's. Her mind was set and nothing would sway her.

'I'm not worried, Devlin.' *Not about that.*

'Good,' he said emphatically. 'Because the more I think about it, the more I realise you were right. We connected on the island, connected in a big way. But it couldn't last for ever.'

'No.' It most certainly couldn't.

His smile almost reached his eyes. 'Even if I have to admit now that I still want you.' His shoulder rolled back. 'We are compatible that way.'

Despite her mindset, she found her wan smile matched his. 'Yes.' They definitely were.

But wait. Had he moved closer? Her skin was beginning to heat again in a dreadfully pleasant way, and her already full breasts were growing heavier by the second.

As their eyes locked more he seemed to read her thoughts and reassured her in that rumbling sexy drawl that never failed to entice, 'Relax, Eden. Just because I want to hold you, doesn't mean I will.'

'You have no intention of kissing me?'

His lidded gaze skimmed her lips and his speculation turned into a sexy smile. 'I didn't until a second ago.'

She hated herself for doing nothing when his hand scooped around her neck and brought her close. Worse, she submitted when he captured her mouth with his. She surrendered totally and she couldn't deny the reason why. A subversive part of her was celebrating, and as it rejoiced the ache of want and wonder only grew.

Accepting his kiss now felt like the most natural and needful thing she'd ever done.

His thumb circled behind her ear and as his breathing deepened her lips parted more. Her nerve-endings burned with awareness when his other hand cupped her jaw, his hot fingers fanning over her temple, through her hair as a powerful, wonderful pressure built low in her belly.

This was how she was born to feel. He was who she was born to love.

When he softly broke the kiss, his lips stayed close to brush back and forth over hers. She felt his grin, the rumble in his chest.

'Eden, love, you could make a man give up his religion.'

A mighty wave of emotion picked her up then flung her back down.

This was madness. She must tell him now, this minute. Maybe here, away from everything and everyone, a miracle would happen. A thunderbolt might streak out of the night sky and hit him with the concrete knowledge that he was, in fact, in love with her and, on top of that, he was thrilled by the news that they would soon be parents together.

Miracles did happen, right?

She filled her lungs and prayed the right words would come. 'Devlin, please listen to me carefully. I need to tell you something important.'

The consuming fire in his eyes flickered and dimmed before he drew away. 'I know the rules. I didn't break them.' He grinned crookedly. 'Only bent them a little. We're agreed. We want different things. That won't change.'

She shook her head. He was on the wrong track. 'Sometimes things aren't so black and white.'

His gaze intensified. 'Are you saying you want me to kiss you again?'

'I'm saying…Devlin, I'm pregnant.'

He blinked once, slowly. 'Pregnant. With…a *baby*?'

Her smile was lame. 'I certainly hope so.'

'*My* baby.'

She nodded.

The confusion on his face gradually changed to a fearsome darkness. Eyes blazing, he shoved to his feet. 'And you hadn't thought to pick up the phone and do something totally off the wall like let me know?'

Eden bit her lip. So much for the news going down well.

She reached for him, to calm him and balance herself. 'Devlin, I wanted to be sure.'

'As far as I know you're either pregnant or you're not.'

It wasn't that simple.

'The tests are positive. I have all the symptoms.'

But there was more. She needed to tell him about her concerns and the scan set for Saturday. She'd been worried, but alongside the constant churn of anxiety came a profound sense of purpose. This baby was meant to be, and, no matter how Devlin took the news, as long as her child was healthy, that blessing would be more than enough.

He clapped his outer thighs and declared, 'Well, this changes everything.'

Her dread turned to the barest shimmer of hope. 'What do you mean?'

'It changes you and me.'

Eden chanced a tiny smile. Did he mean he didn't need to contain his feelings any more? Was that thunderbolt about to strike? Given the fact he hadn't done anything jerk-worthy like say the baby couldn't be his or *I'm not ready for this*, she was more than willing to listen.

She dropped her chin. 'This changes us how?'

He sat down, scrubbed his jaw and scrubbed it again. 'I think we need to…' He blew out a quick breath. 'Well, I think we should probably get married.'

Her heart seemed to stop at the same time a frightening numbness consumed her body.

He'd asked her to marry him. She'd fantasised about a proposal since their first date three years ago. But in her daydreams he'd looked confident, happy, laughing with joy and relief when she cried out, *Yes, of course I'll marry you!*

He didn't look happy now. His mouth was tight, his jaw too, and a sheen of perspiration had broken on his hairline. And what kind of a proposal was that anyway?

I think we should probably get married.

As an afterthought he took her hand. 'Next month. What do you think?'

Her short laugh was devoid of humour. 'I think you'd rather paint fences standing on one leg for the rest of your life than marry me.'

He dropped her hand. 'Eden, I'm serious.'

'So am I.'

He shot to his feet again, his braced stance almost threatening. She'd never seen him so agitated. 'Isn't this what you wanted? A diamond ring. A white dress. We'll buy them tomorrow. We'll get married and—'

'Regret it for the rest of our lives.'

His eyes turned to cool, glittering stone. 'We're good together. We could make a marriage work.'

He made it sound as if he'd be chained in a quarry for

the rest of his days. Worse, he couldn't see how his I'll-sacrifice-myself-for-the-sake-of-our-child reaction hurt her.

He'd been right. They were black and white. He shunned the idea of settling down while she looked forward to it. When would she learn she could never win Devlin's heart? He was unattainable.

Unwinnable.

Devlin had said his mother should have seen the writing on the wall. Deep down, in a dark place he couldn't bear to look, didn't he pray that she would see the same warning and take heed now? If they married, he would grow to resent it, resent her, and possibly even their child. She couldn't have that. She simply couldn't.

She swallowed against a lump of throbbing emotion. 'You care about me, Devlin?'

His nostrils flared. 'Of course I do.'

If she needed to beg, she would.

'Then, please,' *please,* 'don't ask me again. Let this go.'

She dragged herself to her feet and headed for the exit. His hand on her arm urged her back around.

His chin kicked up. 'You're carrying my child. A child needs his father.'

'I would never stop you from seeing the baby. He'll know we both love him. He doesn't need to grow up knowing that—'

She dropped her head as the raw, inescapable truth hit her squarely in the chest and a sob almost escaped. Devlin didn't love her, and if he didn't now he never would, married or not.

'I would never be unfaithful,' he promised, getting to his feet, 'if that's what's worrying you.'

A tear slid down her cheek. 'And that's supposed to be a consolation?'

'For God's sake,' he growled before he inhaled and gathered himself. 'Eden, what do you want from me?'

'The only thing you can't give.'

His pupils dilated as if an idea had struck. He brought her close. 'Eden, I—'

Heat blazed in her cheeks and she tore free. 'Don't you dare lie to me.' *Don't dare tell me that you love me now.* 'I deserve better than that.'

His face hardened to a deathly calm. 'Think of our child.'

'I am.' She was also thinking about another child, a little boy who'd grown up not believing in love. She would not be responsible for passing on that kind of legacy.

'Life isn't a fairy tale,' he said.

'No. Life is about making choices.'

She'd had the choice not to go away with him but she'd refused to acknowledge it. Now she would make the right choice even if it meant her heart was ripped out.

He ran a hand through his hair and sized her up for a long, tense moment. 'I'll take you home.'

'You have a dinner date.'

'I'll cancel.'

'Don't bother.'

He huffed out a jaded laugh. 'You really think I'm a first-class bastard, don't you?'

'I don't think that at all. I believe one day you'll understand precisely how I feel.'

You'll let yourself fall in love, it just won't be with me.

He seemed to think that through before taking her arm. 'We're going home.'

'No.'

She knew from old—he'd give up eventually.

As she stood her ground he dragged a hand down his face, holding his palm over his mouth before shucking back his shoulders. 'Then let me see that you get a cab.'

Her stomach knotted. He looked so…tormented.

Wanting to cry, she cupped his jaw and tried to reassure him. 'It's okay, Devlin. Really it is.'

As long as their child was healthy, that was all that mattered.

'It's not okay.' His gaze lowered to her waist before he linked his arm through hers and ushered her resolutely to the door. 'But you can bet I'll find a way to make sure it ends up that way.'

CHAPTER SIXTEEN

'THIS shouldn't take long, mate. We'll be on the golf course by ten.'

Staring out of the window of Nate's Alpha Romeo, Devlin dragged himself back from his thoughts. Thoughts of Eden. Thoughts of their unborn child. He'd barely slept or eaten these past days for thinking, then thinking more.

Now he turned his attention from suburban weatherboards and gum trees to his brother. 'I wish you'd told me sooner you weren't feeling well.'

Nate had collected him early for their scheduled golf game, explaining that his doctor had ordered a test relating to stomach problems he'd experienced lately.

Speeding up, Nate beat a red light. 'The GP doesn't think it's anything serious. This scan'll just rule out some possibilities.' He flicked over a smile before turning into a medical centre car park. 'I appreciate you coming along.'

'Amazing what technology can do these days.' Devlin snapped his seat belt as Nate swung into a park. 'They use ultrasounds for pregnancies too, you know.'

'Yeah. I know.' Nate shut down the engine, concentrated on the steering wheel for a deliberative moment, then turned a considering eye on his brother. 'Look, Devlin, if you want to talk anything over…'

Devlin's jaw clenched. 'You know all there is to know.' Opening the door, he swung one long leg out. 'I'm going to be a father and the mother has the good sense to refuse my marriage proposal.'

Nate exhaled. 'It sure can be tricky.'

'What's that?'

Nate pinned him with a knowing look. 'Love.'

Devlin manoeuvred out of the car while Nate did the same. 'Do me a favour. Don't talk to me about the L word.' He shut the door harder than necessary. 'I'm not cut out for it.'

'That's what I thought too, until I found the right one.' Watching the traffic, they crossed the car park towards the centre's doors. 'Just hope one day I'll talk her into marrying me.'

Devlin stopped dead and a lime-green Mini beeped its horn and swerved around him. 'You proposed to Sabrina?'

'Over a quiet romantic dinner the other night. She said she's not ready.'

Entering the building's air-conditioned cool, Devlin blew out a breath. 'The Stone brothers seem to be striking out lately.'

'Sabrina's just scared.' He shrugged one shoulder. 'You know, about committing.'

'What happened to men having the monopoly on that phobia?'

Nate clapped Devlin's back. 'The steep price of equality, my friend.'

Devlin had to admit, 'Marriage is scary enough when there are only adults involved. It's near petrifying when you bring a baby into the mix.'

Moving into the plush waiting lounge, Nate held Devlin's shoulder. 'You're a great brother. I have no doubt you'll be a great father.'

'Dad might've thought the same when our mother was pregnant.'

Eden was right to turn him down. What if he showed the same indifference towards his child that his father had to him? He wouldn't risk his own boy, or girl, enduring that kind of torment…feeling sorry for his mother, losing respect for his father, as well as for himself for being powerless to make things right.

The thought of hurting a kid like that made him physically ill.

He'd told Eden he'd find a solution to their predicament, but he hadn't come up with an answer yet. Still, one must exist. Even if he couldn't quite grasp it, he felt it hovering like a mist on the edges of his consciousness. He just needed a little more time for the curling fog to lift.

Nate indicated a chair in a quiet corner. 'Take a seat while I check in.'

Five minutes later, Devlin was gazing blindly at an opened sports magazine, an ankle resting atop the opposite knee, when Nate returned with a surprise guest.

Setting the magazine aside, Devlin pushed to his feet and rushed a hand through his hair. 'Sabrina? Nate didn't say you'd be here.' He brushed a brotherly kiss against her cheek.

Sabrina's lashes lowered, almost coy. 'I thought I'd surprise him and we could go for coffee afterward.'

Shrugging, Devlin looked to Nate. 'You know what they say. Two's company.'

He wasn't in the mood for a hit anyway. He wasn't in the mood for anything other than mulling over his problem. He wanted to be the best father a man could be. The idea he might be emotionally detached from his children was a crushing notion and had haunted him for years. Could the apple land that close to the tree?

'I'd like you to stay,' Nate said to Devlin, 'if that's okay.'

Feeling like a fifth wheel, but wanting to support Nate if he could, Devlin cocked his head. 'Sure.' A thought made his pulse spike ten clicks. 'This *is* standard, right?' There wasn't anything they weren't telling him?

An awkward pause followed where Sabrina muttered something unintelligible at the floor and Nate threw an arm around Devlin's shoulders and urged him towards a room.

'Everything'll be fine,' Nate assured him. 'You have my word.'

Then why did he feel as if he were about to be fed to the lions?

When he entered the private room, Devlin's blood pressure exploded and he cursed under his breath.

Of all the brainless, gullible...

Why hadn't he guessed? The excuse to get him here, the fact Sabrina had happened to show up, those pregnant women in the reception lounge...

His hands went to his hips. 'What a small world.'

Eden lay on a gurney, face towards a blank screen monitor, a blue sheet over her trunk and legs. The instant she heard his voice, she gasped and sat bolt upright.

'Devlin?' Her eyes, round with shock, slowly narrowed. 'You showing up out the blue can't be coincidence. Not twice in one week.' Her gaze slid to Sabrina. 'Did you set this up?'

'It was my idea,' Nate cut in, stepping up to stand beside his girl. 'Devlin needs to be here today, and it was obvious that wasn't going to happen without a little friendly intervention.'

Sheepish, Sabrina manufactured a short laugh and shrugged. 'The things we do for love.'

Exhaling, Devlin dusted his hands and moved forward. Now he was here, no use pretending he wasn't interested. Wasn't every day he walked in on the woman who shrank from the idea of marrying him but who was also about to undergo an ultrasound of his firstborn.

He lifted his chin at the monitor. 'I take it this is a routine procedure?'

Eden blinked several times and her face seemed to pale more. 'Pretty much.'

Devlin glanced between the three culpable faces—Eden, Nate, Sabrina—and all sorts of cruddy notions went through his mind, such as he wasn't the father of Eden's baby after all and this was their weird way of breaking the news. Then, piggybacking on an earlier thought, another idea descended and his chest tightened so much that he flinched.

'Is there something wrong with…?'

The last words stuck in his throat. His heart was pounding, a thumping roar against his ribs. Good Lord, and he'd thought he knew all there was to know about stress.

His plea came out a husky croak. 'Eden…tell me.'

'I had some spotting last week,' Eden admitted, her cheeks flaming more. 'It's not so uncommon. Women have scans at twelve weeks anyway. Everything'll be okay.'

The backs of his knees caved in. Devlin fell into a chair near her bed and, elbows on knees, cradled his forehead. After a few moments he got out, 'Why didn't you tell me?'

'I didn't want you to worry.'

'So you took all the worry on yourself?'

'I know he'll be all right.'

Devlin took her cool hand and, assuring her with his eyes, squeezed. 'I know it too.'

Gathering himself, he straightened and cleared his throat. He'd meant what he'd said. Everything would be fine. They should focus on practicalities. Be positive.

'Is there anything else you need?' he asked. 'There must be medical expenses.'

Her eyes glistened as she softly smiled. 'We have time to sort that out.'

A tall woman with a dark bob strolled in. 'Morning.' She nodded at Eden. 'I'm the sonographer taking care of you this morning. Are you ready to see some amazing pictures?'

Sabrina bent to kiss Eden's cheek. 'Time we bowed out.'

Nate shook Devlin's hand. 'Good luck, mate.'

The ultrasound technician sat on a stool near equipment that looked very much like a home computer system—a monitor, keyboard and hard drive. She acknowledged Devlin with a cheery smile. 'You're the lucky dad?'

He nodded firmly. 'That would be me.'

'Well, mum-to-be,' the woman said to Eden, 'let's get started.'

After lowering the sheet and applying gel to Eden's exposed skin, the woman slid a sensor firmly over her patient's lower abdominal area. A black-and-white image flickered onto the screen. Pulse beating high in his throat, Devlin edged closer at the same time his jaw unhinged.

Amazing was right.

The sonographer explained, 'Ultrasounds use high-frequency sound waves and their echoes to create three-dimensional images which are constantly updated, so the scan shows your baby's movements. We can check the position of the placenta and the gestational age too.'

A head swam onto the screen, the little body, legs, arms, even fingers!

'That's him?' Devlin asked, overcome by a surreal sensation that left him tingling.

'Or her,' Eden pointed out in a dreamy voice.

'It's a little early to predict gender,' the woman let them know. 'I don't want to disappoint anyone.'

He and Eden said together, 'We won't be disappointed.'

They shared a glance, smiled, and Devlin held her hand in both of his.

'Is that the heartbeat?' he asked, focusing on a small pulsing light.

The woman held the sensor still. 'Certainly is. And performing exactly how it should. Great news. I'll just take some measurements now, but everything's looking good.'

For the next few wondrous moments, they studied the incredible moving images while the woman measured and pinpointed dates.

Some time during the examination, Devlin's gaze wandered from the monitor to the mother of his child. So vulnerable and beautiful and totally committed to the image on the screen—to his baby...their family.

A sweeping emotion spiralled up through him, something acute he'd never felt before. It was like feeling responsible for the sun rising on a perfectly clear day, or suddenly being able to reach out and touch the moon.

Had he consciously fought it? He wasn't certain. All he knew was he couldn't deny it. Here was the answer. He wanted this, more than air he wanted to be part of what he had here and felt now—every day, every hour for the rest of his life.

His throat thick, he moved closer until his lips brushed the shell of her ear.

'God, I love you.'

Eden swung her attention from the screen to Devlin and mentally shook her head. She hadn't heard right. She couldn't have done.

'What did you say?'

His eyes were uncommonly soft. 'I love you.'

She blinked rapidly.

Eden, don't get excited. Clearly this was an adjunct to the other night. He'd been about to say those same words after he'd proposed. *I love you* was just another way to work his charm and get what he wanted. To get her back in his bed and also have his child under his roof, for better or for worse.

Her voice lowered. She didn't want the sonographer to hear. 'We've been through this.'

'I don't think we have.' His smile was almost boyish. 'At least *I* haven't.'

She inspected his brow for signs of fever. 'Are you feeling okay?'

'I feel…' he pressed a kiss to her hand '…*fantastic.*'

Eden looked to the technician who, smiling, waved it off. 'Visual stimulus is extremely powerful. It sometimes gets new dads this way.' She rose and moved towards the door. 'I'll give you two a moment alone.'

Devlin shunted his chair closer as Eden sat slowly up.

'The other night,' he said, 'when I proposed, you thought I'd asked out of a sense of duty. I won't lie…there

is a sense of duty, but there's more. There's a sense of…
well, destiny.'

Eden sucked in a breath.

This sounded too good. It couldn't be real. She didn't
want to believe too much, hope too hard.

Nevertheless, she bit her lip as unshed tears stung
behind her nose. 'Please, don't say what you don't mean.'

'But you know that I do mean it. I'd be a raving fool not
to face the fact that if I don't make you my wife, I'll be mis-
erable for the rest of my life. I want to keep you both safe.'
He stopped, then tilted his head as if something had
clicked. 'The not-so-crazy part is, if you let me do that I
think I'll finally be safe too.'

Her throat ached with a mix of happiness and fear. 'But
what if you regret it? What about your adventures?'

But she saw only strength and truth gleaming in his
eyes. 'Do you honestly think that matters any more? Besides, we'll have our own adventures, the biggest and best
raising a family of our own.'

He held her cheek and spoke close to her lips, his voice
deep and determined.

'I'm sure about this. About you and me. I'm not my
father. Took me the long way round to realise that. To
realise that I won't be happy, and neither will you, unless
we're together.'

A happy, hopeful sob bubbled up in her throat.
'You're sure?'

His smile lit his eyes. 'It's wonderful knowing for certain. Exciting yet…peaceful.'

She turned more, set her palm against his chest and felt
his heart beat as his eyes searched hers with an earnestness
that made her shiver with the purest sense of longing.

'Eden, let us all win this time. Tell me you feel the same way.'

Her voice was the barest, thankful whisper. 'You must know that I do.'

'Then you'll marry me?'

She searched his beautiful eyes. 'Yes.' *Oh, yes!* 'I love you, Devlin.'

I'll love you till the end of time.

He gathered her close and held her for a protracted, tender moment, as though he might crush her if he embraced her too tightly or she might disappear if he dared let her go.

Trembling with unsurpassed joy, she murmured against his jaw, 'Devlin?'

He came away. His knuckle and adoring gaze curved her jaw. 'Yes, love?'

She smiled and a tear sped down her cheek. 'We've wasted so much time.'

'We'll make up for it, starting now.'

When his warm, soft lips covered hers, Eden thought she heard angels sing. And she knew…knew for certain and with all her heart.

She wrapped her arms around his neck.

Then she kissed him back.

EPILOGUE

Dear Diary,

I can't believe last week marked another wonderful wedding anniversary! Devlin and I have been married four thoroughly blissful years. Even better...today Sabrina and Nate were married too.

Nate looked so proud and confident standing at the head of the church, hands loosely clasped before him as he waited for his beautiful bride to walk down the garland-laced aisle. But, as chief bridesmaid, peeking around the corner seconds before the bridal march began, I couldn't keep my eyes off the handsome best man, in that dark blue suit, black hair neat, twilight eyes smouldering back at me.

I was wondering how I could contain my gratitude and love from spilling over into tears when I felt a tug on my skirt and looked down.

Beside me stood the prettiest, and bravest, flower girl God ever created. The hem of her white organza dress touched her satin slippers while her trademark blond curls cascaded from beneath a ring of pale pink roses. In her slightly trembling hand, she held a long-handled white wicker basket.

As I kissed her cheek the music started and Lonnie headed off, announcing, 'Don't worry, Mummy. I'll do good.'

Walking behind her, I held my bouquet and beamed as Lonnie sprinkled petals from her basket just as Sabrina and I had taught her in rehearsal. The guests in the pews sighed and it was clear from the devoted look in her father's eyes that Devlin, too, prized our little girl more than anything in this world.

At the wedding reception, Lonnie wanted to dance, so Devlin swung her up and swayed with her to a ballad, chuckling whenever she cupped her sweet dimpled hand around his jaw to kiss his cheek.

Wanting to join in, I crossed from the overflowing gift table to the dance floor and asked my sparky three-and-a-half-year-old, 'Do I get to dance with the best man? He is my date, after all.'

I winked at Devlin, who grinned and winked back.

'Mummy!' Lonnie cried as she twirled in her father's arms and saw me. 'We'll all dance!'

But when the cute ring boy scurried past, Lonnie forgot about her parents and kicked to be free. Devlin lowered her carefully then wrapped those same strong arms around me.

The feeling never changes. Always safe.

Always loved.

His adoring gaze held mine as he rocked me gently and his warm fingers brushed my temple.

'It's a funny thing,' he said.

My brows nudged together. 'What's funny?'

'I didn't think I could love you any more than on the day we were married, but it keeps getting stronger. Keeps getting better.'

Drinking in the wonderful moment, I let my heart answer for me. 'I know exactly what you mean.'

He smiled over at the flower girl sitting on the floor with the ring boy near the cake table. 'Lonnie did good today.'

I remembered Lonnie's words before she'd headed off with her basket of petals and I grinned. 'She's her father's daughter.'

'She has her mother's hair.'

'But your eyes.'

'And your big heart.' His broad shoulders squared. 'Let's have another one.'

We'd never discussed falling pregnant for a second time. Not wanting to push, willing to wait, I'd wanted Devlin to bring the subject up. Now I was so surprised, and pleased, I almost buckled.

'So, you're ready to do it now?' I asked.

'Well, sure.' He rested his forehead upon mine. 'Could get tricky leaving in the middle of the reception though.'

I laughed and, laughing too, he spun me around. My husband's smiles are the only wings I need to fly.

'Where's your adventurous spirit?' I teased, dizzy from both our twirl and the depth of my love for him.

He took my hand and placed it on his chest. 'Right here, and it's all yours.'

Beneath the slow-spinning lights, with other couples dancing nearby, he kissed me and I knew as I'd never known before.

Devlin Stone and I don't merely have time…we have the rest of eternity—for our love, for our family—and you can bet Cupid's arrow we'll make the most of every minute.

XOXO

Bestselling Harlequin Presents author

Lynne Graham

brings you an exciting new miniseries:

PREGNANT BRIDES

Inexperienced and expecting, they're forced to marry

Collect them all:

DESERT PRINCE, BRIDE OF INNOCENCE
January 2010

RUTHLESS MAGNATE, CONVENIENT WIFE
February 2010

GREEK TYCOON, INEXPERIENCED MISTRESS
March 2010

TWO CROWNS, TWO ISLANDS, ONE LEGACY

A royal family torn apart by pride and its lust for power, reunited by purity and passion

Harlequin Presents is proud to bring you the final two installments from The Royal House of Karedes. As the stories unfold, secrets and sins from the past are revealed and desire, love and passion war with royal duty!

Look for:

RUTHLESS BOSS, ROYAL MISTRESS
by Natalie Anderson
January 2010

THE DESERT KING'S HOUSEKEEPER BRIDE
by Carol Marinelli
February 2010

www.eHarlequin.com

HP12883

REQUEST YOUR FREE BOOKS!

2 FREE NOVELS PLUS 2 FREE GIFTS!

YES! Please send me 2 FREE Harlequin Presents® novels and my 2 FREE gifts (gifts are worth about $10). After receiving them, if I don't wish to receive any more books, I can return the shipping statement marked "cancel". If I don't cancel, I will receive 6 brand-new novels every month and be billed just $4.05 per book in the U.S. or $4.74 per book in Canada. That's a savings of close to 15% off the cover price! It's quite a bargain! Shipping and handling is just 50¢ per book*. I understand that accepting the 2 free books and gifts places me under no obligation to buy anything. I can always return a shipment and cancel at any time. Even if I never buy another book, the two free books and gifts are mine to keep forever.

106 HDN EYRQ 306 HDN EYR2

Name	(PLEASE PRINT)	
Address		Apt. #
City	State/Prov.	Zip/Postal Code

Signature (if under 18, a parent or guardian must sign)

Mail to the **Harlequin Reader Service:**
IN U.S.A.: P.O. Box 1867, Buffalo, NY 14240-1867
IN CANADA: P.O. Box 609, Fort Erie, Ontario L2A 5X3

Not valid to current subscribers of Harlequin Presents books.

Are you a current subscriber of Harlequin Presents books and want to receive the larger-print edition? Call 1-800-873-8635 today!

* Terms and prices subject to change without notice. Prices do not include applicable taxes. Sales tax applicable in N.Y. Canadian residents will be charged applicable provincial taxes and GST. Offer not valid in Quebec. This offer is limited to one order per household. All orders subject to approval. Credit or debit balances in a customer's account(s) may be offset by any other outstanding balance owed by or to the customer. Please allow 4 to 6 weeks for delivery. Offer available while quantities last.

Your Privacy: Harlequin Books is committed to protecting your privacy. Our Privacy Policy is available online at www.eHarlequin.com or upon request from the Reader Service. From time to time we make our lists of customers available to reputable third parties who may have a product or service of interest to you. If you would prefer we not share your name and address, please check here. ☐

HP09R

I ♥

HARLEQUIN® *Presents*

BROUGHT TO YOU BY FANS OF
HARLEQUIN PRESENTS.

We are its editors and authors
and biggest fans—and we'd
love to hear from YOU!

**Subscribe today to our online blog at
www.iheartpresents.com**